D1715144

A STORY OF REDEMPTION, ADOPTION, AND HOPE

Kim Ray Mishler

WESTBOW
PRESS®
A DIVISION OF THOMAS NELSON
& ZONDERVAN

WestBow Press books may be ordered through booksellers or by contacting:

WestBow Press
A Division of Thomas Nelson & Zondervan
1663 Liberty Drive
Bloomington, IN 47403
www.westbowpress.com
1 (866) 928-1240

ISBN: 978-1-9736-3185-9 (sc)
ISBN: 978-1-9736-3187-3 (hc)
ISBN: 978-1-9736-3186-6 (e)

Library of Congress Control Number: 2018907373

Print information available on the last page.

WestBow Press rev. date: 7/19/2018

The LORD says,
"I will rescue those who love me.
I will protect those who trust in my name."
Psalm 91:14(NLT)

Dedicated to:
My beautiful daughter Hannah

Acknowledgment

I awoke one spring morning in May 2016 with a story forming in my mind. I couldn't rest until I sat down and began to write. There was no breakfast that morning as I was being spoon-fed a story by God. We had such a lovely time together as the story began to take shape. Even so, I still questioned whether this was something He wanted me to do. He affirmed it the next day with a small herd of does in my backyard. As you read you will understand why deer grazing in my yard was significant.

God gave me the story, He affirmed it in miraculous ways, and He sent me many helpers to bring the story to life. I couldn't have written this without their valuable input, and I am eternally grateful.

To my helpers:

Whether you could identify with one of my characters and helped me see into their souls, provided factual perspective or took the time to edit and proofread, I thank you.

Tonya H., your personal and professional experiences helped me know that I was on track in those very early stages. *Steph*, you gave me a reality check that helped me develop my main character and fall more deeply in love with her.

Jennifer, your encouragement and insight into secondary characters drove me to develop their positions further. Janelle, you challenged me with plot twists and have been my number one prayer support, and I am so thankful for your encouragement.

Christi, Janie, and Tricia, you all could identify with the book in various ways that might be different from others who read it. Your willingness to read it and give me feedback means the world.

Vicki, your open and honest thoughts completely changed the first chapter of the book, and I can't even begin to tell you what a gift that was to me and to the story. Karen, you added much wisdom as an adoptive mom and foster mom. Thank you both for your prayers and empowering me to move forward.

Melinda, you read it from the perspective of a young woman who has not experienced any of the hard topics mentioned in the book and gave me insight into how it would be received from someone in your age group, background, etc. You are a sweetheart for blessing your Auntie in this way! And thanks to your mom Jane, and sisters Megan and Molly, who read it alongside you. Briana, thank you for being my clean-up crew! You were so helpful.

Brenda, you not only gave your personal time and professional talents to the book, but you guided me, advised me and picked me up when it seemed overwhelming. I appreciate your wisdom. Last, but not least, to my wonderful husband Joel, who sat down and read the novel amidst his busy schedule, not once, but twice! You gave valuable insight, and I wrote additional chapters that enhanced the story because of your suggestions. You pushed me towards publishing because you believe in the message of the story. We share a passion for life and have been recipients of the beautiful gift of adoption; an unselfish act of love that changed our lives forever.

Thanks to all of you who have given your time, talent, input, encouragement and prayers. You were my rescuers during the process giving me the courage to move forward. I am blessed.

CHAPTER One

Krista fell to her knees and wrapped her arms tightly around her mother's legs. "Don't leave us here, Momma, please!" she begged between sobs. Without saying a word, Momma pried Krista's hands off her and turned quickly toward the exit.

"Just take us with you this time," Erin pleaded as she watched her mother close the door to the rooftop fire escape. It was no use. Their momma was gone. Once again, the girls were left alone. The rooftop of their apartment building that had been their playground over the last six months was now their hiding place.

Mandy Lewis stood there with her arms around her two younger sisters, consoling them and devising a plan for how she would ease the pain of being left behind this time around.

Blinking back her tears, Mandy pulled the girls close to her. She was mature for her 13 years. She had to be. It had become clear to her over the years that she had to protect her younger sisters. This wasn't the first time their mother had left them in what she called, "a hiding place", until she could find a place for them to stay. Getting evicted from one place to another, their momma made it a practice to find a hiding place where no one would notice her absence from the children and report them to the authorities. The girls never understood why they couldn't just go with their mother to look for a place to stay, nor did their mother bother giving them an explanation. She would simply say to them, "sit tight and stay out of trouble until I return." Sometimes she would return in a few hours, but sometimes it would get quite late into the night before she would come for them. Mandy could see by her sisters' expressions that they were afraid to spend the night on the rooftop.

Secretly, Mandy feared it too.

"It won't be so bad, this time," Mandy promised, trying to sound upbeat. "We'll have a rooftop picnic with the sandwiches Momma made for us." Squeezing their shoulders, she added, "After that, we'll lay on our blanket and look for cloud creatures in the sky!"

8-year-old Krista caught on to Mandy's excitement. Her whimpering quieted. She loved the idea of a game.

Even though she was just a year older than Krista, Erin wasn't as easily persuaded. "Why can't we wait inside at Miss Roger's apartment, or down in the lobby or something? How long is she going to leave us out here on the roof?"

"I don't know, Erin. I never know. But it is a nice day out here and look at all the fluffy clouds in the sky!" Mandy tried again to direct Erin's focus elsewhere.

Erin folded her arms and stomped over to the blanket her mother had spread out for them. She plopped herself down, leaning up against the garbage bag sitting on the corner that held their meager belongings. "I hope we don't have to change schools again, I hate it when we change schools."

"Me too," Krista chimed in. "I like my school; my teacher is nice." She left Mandy's side and found a seat on the blanket next to her sister. They sat there, side by side, sad and alone and Mandy's heart was filled with sorrow for all of them. The same questions Mandy asked many times were racing through her mind. How can

Momma do this to us again? Are we going to be on the run our whole lives?

Will we ever have a real home?

The roar of a distant lawn mower jolted Mandy back from the rooftop days to present reality. She stretched and took a deep breath, as if trying to free herself from the weight of this childhood memory.

"We never did get a real home," she whispered as she exhaled. Mandy blinked hard and shifted her gaze toward the blue spring sky. When memories of her sisters and their childhood surfaced, it was easier to just push them back into the recesses of her mind. She had not seen Erin and Krista in years. She desperately missed them but hoped their lives had turned out better than hers. So many things had changed in Mandy's life since that rooftop moment with her frightened sisters. The last time she spoke to them, they were happy living with their dad, Hank. While she was happy for them, she envied them. Mandy never knew her dad and never had a place she could call home. She was certain though, if she ever did have a home, it would have a front porch like the one she was relaxing on.

This front porch had become her refuge in the last few months of her life. Fragrant lilac bushes lined the banister and hummingbirds danced at feeders hanging from poles. They were just simple things, but to Mandy, they were paradise. She nestled deeper into her chair and took in the gorgeous morning. She couldn't take her eyes off the billowy clouds in the sea of blue above her. She blamed the sky for the childhood memories. When she saw fluffy clouds, she was always reminded of Erin and Krista.

The rooftop excursion she remembered wasn't the only one she had as a child. She and her sisters often viewed clouds from their apartment rooftops. They laid side by side with their arms linked and pointed out shapes in the clouds. Sometimes they did it for fun. Other times, they did it as a diversion while they waited. The three girls had learned to be creative when their mother was gone.

Mandy and her sisters lived like Nomads, moving from low cost housing to foster homes. Their mother's addiction to heroin was the driving force that governed their lives. When Mandy was 16 years old, her mother went too far in her quest to obtain the poison that controlled her. She put her daughters' lives at risk and went to prison. Erin and Krista were reunited with their dad. Mandy was sent to North Hampton Group Home for Girls.

The courtyard at North Hampton was Mandy's first introduction to the pleasures of nature. It was filled with trees and brightly colored zinnias that grew along the walkway. The tranquility of the courtyard comforted Mandy during some lonely days during her high school years. The courtyard is where she took solace on the weekends when her roommates visited their family members.

After graduation from high school Mandy had to say goodbye to the courtyard, and those who had cared for her at North Hampton Group Home for Girls. On her own, with no one to call family, she rented a room above a local pawn shop that was within walking distance of her job at a factory. With its sparse furnishings, shared bathroom and musty smell, it lacked any resemblance of tranquility. She knew it was temporary, just like all the other places she had lived in her life, but it met her needs and she felt safe there. She was finding her way in life and gaining confidence until a string of bad choices caused her to lose it all. Over the last several months she had experienced hopelessness because of those choices. However, it was because of those choices she had come to this new sanctuary, the front porch where she found rest.

She closed her eyes and allowed the warm sun to kiss her cheeks as the gentle breeze teased the wisps of hair that fell from her long dark braid. For the first time in her life, Mandy Lewis felt at peace.

Mandy always loved spring because it meant the end of long, hard winters where she and her family battled the cold, snowy Indiana climate. But this spring signified more than just an end to a cold winter--it was the end of a long, hard journey and the beginning of a new one. Even though she knew the journey ahead of her would be the hardest one she would ever take; it was a journey she was destined to make. Moments from the past few months flashed through Mandy's mind and she found her eyes growing wet again.

Tears were always close to the surface these days, prompted by a variety of different emotions. Today, they fell freely with thoughts of determination, renewed hope, and a peace that she never knew before. It was the peace she had read about in her Bible that morning. It came from Philippians 4:7 (NIV) which says, "*And the peace of God, which passes all understanding, will guard your hearts and your thoughts in Christ Jesus.*" It was this peace she was discovering through a personal relationship with Jesus Christ that she needed right now. Mandy staked her claim deep in the soil of this verse and was determined to take refuge in this promise in the days ahead.

Warmed by the morning sun and lost in her thoughts, Mandy drifted off to sleep. The singing birds seemed to be humming a lullaby and soon Mandy was dreaming. She had the recurring dream that haunted her over the past few months. It was also the dream that had played a distinct role in the life changing decisions she recently made.

In her dream, Mandy is walking through a forest, thick with trees and brush and the sounds of creatures she can't identify. At every turn, she becomes entangled in the mass of hanging branches and undergrowth. She ventures further and further from the light and darkness creeps in around her. Her heart races as she tries desperately to find her way out of the maze of trees.

She is startled by the scurry of something in the bushes behind her. Instinctively, she turns to find herself eye to eye with a massive doe. Mandy catches her breath and is paralyzed with fear. However, the doe is not startled by the sight of her. Their eyes lock. The doe's big brown eyes pierce deep into Mandy's soul. They are filled with pain and sorrow. Mandy is so moved by the sadness in the doe's eyes that she feels compelled to reach out and console her. The doe flinches at her touch, but Mandy doesn't give up. She lays her hand on her neck and gently strokes her soft fur. The doe releases a low groan that seems to come from deep within her heart. The sound doesn't frighten Mandy yet draws her in more. She senses the doe has immense grief. Although it is strange to connect with an animal, Mandy feels as if their souls touch. Mandy understands that this gentle creature is heartbroken. There is something about the doe that endears her to Mandy and she is filled with empathy and compassion.

As if she is part of a science-fiction fairytale, Mandy feels an urgency to stay with the doe. The doe makes a move and Mandy follows alongside her with eagerness. The doe takes the lead and they walk side by side through the forest. Mandy realizes that she isn't afraid of the forest anymore. She is strangely comforted by following the doe through the forest. It is the doe's domain, after all, and Mandy feels safe by her side.

Mandy felt like the doe's movements were intentional, that she was deliberately leading her somewhere. She walked with purpose and determination but was careful not to get ahead of Mandy. Mandy whispered, "Where are we going, girl?" The sound of crunching leaves underfoot was interrupted by the roar of rushing water. The doe's steps quickened with a sense of urgency as she rushed towards the source of the water. Mandy was short of breath and finding it difficult to keep up. She feared losing her if she decided to run.

The doe stopped as if to wait on Mandy, looking back at her and pawing the ground with urgency, signaling Mandy to pick up the pace. Mandy broke into a jog only for the doe to take off again quickly as they approached a river. In the distance, Mandy saw a pile of rocks that formed a roughhewn circle on the river bank.

The doe made a full sprint toward the rock pile. Keeping the doe in her sights, Mandy dashed to catch up to her. She saw the doe pacing around the rocks, pawing the ground, putting her nose to the sand and acting peculiar. Mandy was fearful of where the doe had led her and what she might find, but she trusted her completely.

Breathless, Mandy arrived at the rock pile. The loud, nervous panting of the doe seemed louder than the roar of the river. She was clearly in a state of panic. Mandy approached the rock pile with caution, peering carefully in. Then, she saw it…the source of the poor doe's despair.

"Mandy, Mandy, wake up!" Startled, Mandy woke up abruptly to find her roommate, Rae, looking at her with concern.

"You were having the dream again, weren't you?" Rae asked.

Mandy nodded. She looked at her sweet friend and said, "Yes, but it doesn't seem as scary anymore".

Rae stretched out her hand to assist Mandy from her comfy spot on the front porch.

Mandy accepted her friend's help and stood up as straight as her bulging stomach would let her. She felt a little kick from inside her belly. Just as she had reached out to console the doe in her dreams, she now reached down to comfort the baby growing inside of her.

CHAPTER Two

The aroma of freshly brewed coffee and hot buttered cinnamon toast lingered in Ayala's kitchen, as did the crumbs on her countertop. Ayala brushed the crumbs into her hand with quick movement and put them in the trash. She was glad her houseguests cleaned up after themselves, but her neat and tidy personality wished they would be more thorough. Ayala looked heavenward and said a quick prayer for patience followed by a prayer of thanksgiving that God had sent two special young ladies into her life. "If a few crumbs are all it costs me, God, then it's well worth the mess," she breathed out as she gave the countertop a quick swipe with the dish rag.

Though adjusting to houseguests wasn't easy, Ayala was confident they were sent to her for a special purpose. Having them around helped fill the painful void left behind after her husband's death. She missed Tim. She ached for his touch, his voice, and even his loud snoring at night. The good and the bad – she missed it all. Although Tim had been gone for over a year now, she still loved him with every ounce of her being. She owed so much to him. She often referred to him as her rescuer and he would playfully respond by puffing out his chest and flexing his muscles. Then, he'd swoop her up in a strong embrace, kiss her on the neck and remind her that he wasn't the rescuer. He was just the person God used to get the job done.

He was right. She was on a path of destruction before she met him. It was his job as a police officer to rescue people. But he had done more than just physically rescue her. He had introduced her to the rescuer of her soul – Jesus Christ. If he had not introduced her to a personal relationship with Jesus Christ, she didn't know where her life would have taken her. She did know one thing for sure; she would not be feeling the pain of his absence right now. Losing Tim hurt, but the joy she experienced in their thirty-year journey together far outweighed the pain of his death. There was great comfort in knowing she'd see him again one day. Eternal life in heaven is the reward for those that call on Jesus to be their Savior. The assurance of knowing she'd see Tim in heaven again one day gave her peace. Ayala longed for this day, but until then, she was fueled by the love of Christ who filled her earthly days with hope and purpose. Tim reminded her over the years of the big plans God had for her. Now, in Tim's absence, she would keep busy learning what those plans were.

Ayala promised Tim in their last precious days together that she wouldn't sit and grieve but would carry on the work she believed God created her to do. Tim's favorite bible verse was: *For we are God's handiwork, created in Christ Jesus to do good works, which God prepared in advance for us to do, Ephesians 2:10.* This verse set the standard by which Tim Banks lived his life. He modeled this principle for Ayala from day one of their relationship until his last breath. He used it to shine light on her darkest day, thirty-three years ago, when she was at the lowest point of her life. At that point in her life, the idea of being God's handiwork was the furthest thing from her mind. On her first encounter with Tim he told her about eternal life. A prisoner to the sin in her life, Ayala was desperate for good news. Tim shared with her how Jesus died on the cross to save her from her selfish and sinful ways. He introduced her to Jesus Christ who forgave her and set her free from the bondage that enslaved her. As she grew in her relationship with Christ she learned that she was, indeed, God's handiwork. Even though Tim would no longer be there to cheer her on, she had promised him she would continue God's good work.

That promise is why she carried her hand-crafted sign that displayed Ephesians 2:10 outside the local abortion clinic. Several days a week she went there and prayed for the women approaching the clinic doors. She prayed they would see her Ephesians sign and know that they and their unborn child are truly God's handiwork created with a purpose. She wanted them to know what she wished she had known many years ago; every person is custom designed by God.

Some days, standing on the concrete sidewalk in the cold Indiana winters was burdensome. Her feet and ankles would hurt. She often found herself to be less tolerant of pro-choice supporters who approached her and her praying friends. They declared that women have a right to choose what they do with their bodies because of the freedom they have living in the United States. Ayala knew all about freedom from her own personal experience of being set free in Christ from the captivity of sin. Because of this, Ayala didn't think these supporters could possibly understand what true freedom really felt like. Ayala did not want a young woman learning about true freedom when it was too late, as she had. This work she was doing at the abortion clinic was personal and any suffering endured was worth it.

Ayala gulped down the last sip of her coffee and drafted a quick note to her house guests telling them that she had a meeting at church this evening and that dinner would be at seven o'clock.

CHAPTER Three

Professor Johnson furrowed his brow and tapped his toe, while Rae Carver clumsily rummaged through her purse to find the ringing phone that was interrupting his class.

Embarrassed, Rae grabbed the phone and quickly hit the button on the side to silence the ringer. She noticed that the word "Dad" flashed on the front screen. "I'm sorry Professor Johnson," Rae murmured, her eyes downcast. "It won't happen again." She nervously clicked her mechanical pencil, noting that it needed more lead.

Professor Johnson cleared his throat and passed out a stack of papers. "This quiz," he announced, "is thirty percent of your grade."

When Rae saw that the quiz was multiple choice, she was relieved. Oh, the irony, she mused to herself. Multiple choice. More decision making.

Lately, it seemed Rae's life was one big quiz filled with multiple choice questions and she consistently failed at circling the correct answers. It seemed the only things she was successfully mastering in her junior year of college were bad choices. It didn't take long into the quiz for Rae to figure out that the trend would continue. She took a deep breath and began to randomly mark answers on the paper hoping she circled enough right responses to pass.

Not only was she struggling to complete the exam, she was worried about the voicemail she assumed her dad had left from her unanswered call.

Rae was certain her dad was going to question her grades and give her a well-rehearsed lecture on the importance of keeping up her grade point average to support her scholarship. Her grades were recently slipping, and she had managed to dodge a string of calls and texts from him and her mother by saying she was busy studying or at an event where she couldn't speak.

Rae simply did not have the courage to face them with the truth. The last few months had been filled with one challenge after another for Rae and she knew her mom would hear it in her voice. Sometimes, Rae wondered if her mom invented the term "mother's intuition". It seemed she knew Rae better than she knew herself. As a child, when Rae washed her grandmother's ring down the sink, when she kissed Billy Walker on the playground, or when her best friend Sadie hurt her feelings, her mother always knew, no matter how hard Rae tried to cover it up. Her mom always seemed to have a solution to her dilemmas, or the appropriate discipline to set her straight. It's one of the many reasons Rae loved and admired her mom so much. Her mother instinctively knew what to do and say. Rae's dream was to be as sure and confident as her mom someday.

Of all the times Rae needed her mom's wisdom, it was now. She longed to lay her head on her mother's lap and hear her say everything would be okay. Her sweet momma always knew what to do and Rae knew she could solve her current situation too. As much as she longed for her mom to fix this for her, she feared disappointing her more.

Her parents, Rick and Nancy Carver, had stood by Rae and her brother, Kurt, no matter what they did. They partnered in nurturing, mentoring and encouraging their children throughout all the ups and downs of childhood. What Rae valued most, however, was that her parents taught her and Kurt about the love of Jesus and the power of prayer. They lived their love of Jesus out for all to see and if Rae was sure about anything in this world – it was that Rick and Nancy Carver loved Jesus and each other. They were leaders in their church, their community and in Rae's life. They had nudged her where she needed a push, held her back when she needed time and gave her a reality check many times over. But always, Rick and Nancy Carver pointed their daughter to Jesus.

Rick was proud when Rae accepted a scholarship to his alma mater and decided to follow in his footsteps in the field of pharmaceuticals. Rae's love of the pharmacy began when she posed as her dad's pharmacy sidekick at the age of four. When her mother, Nancy, was on bed rest while pregnant with Kurt, her dad took her to work with him to their family owned pharmacy. Rae mimicked her dad, wearing an oversized lab coat and playing for hours with bottles, beakers and measuring spoons her dad gave her. She mixed, measured, and pretended to help her make-believe customers all day. Her love for the field of pharmaceuticals grew throughout her life. She worked in the pharmacy, under her dad's mentoring, serving as a pharmacy attendant during high school. Rick had big dreams of Rae being his partner one day and eventually taking over the family business. He even presented her with a lab coat complete with her embroidered name under the Carver Family Pharmacy logo at her college sendoff party, making a big speech about his future hopes and dreams for her and the family business.

Rae adored her parents. Therefore, she could not tell her parents yet about the mess she was in. She could not disappoint them and dash their dreams and plans for her. They had done so much for her and she feared letting them down. She was ashamed to look them in the eye and tell them how one bad choice after another had put her in a place where their dreams for her would not happen. She could not tell them how their daughter, who had earned an academic scholarship to one of Indiana's most prestigious universities, had blown it all away and changed the course of her future forever.

She could not tell them. Not yet.

CHAPTER Four

Mandy left the doctor's office with an excellent report. During prenatal checkups, hearing her baby girl's heartbeat was always something to look forward to. But ultrasounds were the best. Seeing her daughter formed perfectly and relaxed in her cozy waterbed made Mandy's heart swell. She wondered how her baby would look. Would she have dark hair like hers? Would they share the same hazel eyes? Or would she have sparkling blue starbursts for eyes, like those of Kade Dean?

Oh, the mere thought of Kade Dean made her go weak in the knees. She had looked deep into those sparkling blue eyes of his and felt a connection she had never experienced. Those eyes pierced right down into her soul, taking down the walls of mistrust she had spent a lifetime building around her heart. How could she have misread him? How could she have been so foolish as to lose her resolve with him? She had spent many sleepless nights wondering why she thought she could trust him.

Before meeting Kade, Mandy had prided herself on being conscientious. Because of her painful childhood, she had learned to approach everything and everyone with caution. She was a survivor with a plan, ready for any circumstance. She was street smart, able to size up a situation before moving forward. Her survivor skills weren't just something she learned; they were a necessity. Her drug-addicted mother had left Mandy and her sisters alone so many times that instinctively she had fulfilled the roles of mother and protector many times over.

Together, the sisters had survived frequent hunger and recurring episodes of head lice and bedbugs. They had slept with roaches and rats, on hard floors and with the cold drafts of winter whistling through their windows. They lay awake many nights huddled together, listening to the sirens and the sounds of the city and wondering if they'd ever see their mother again. Even as a child, she learned who she could trust and, most importantly, who she could not.

Mother had left them alone plenty, but it didn't stop Mandy from loving her. She remembered laughter and fun times with her when she wasn't high or absent from their life. Her mother was frugal, always able to make a meal out of their inadequate supply. She was resourceful in making up games for them to play and would join in on the fun when the three sisters were very young.

As the girls grew, so did their mother's drug habit. Mandy's heart also grew in its longing to know her as the fun-loving mom she used to be. She longed for her mother to stroke her hair, or giggle under the covers with her as they watched Saturday-morning cartoons together. Over the years, laughter and admiration slowly succumbed to fear and instability, and it became increasingly clear that she could not rely on her mother. The only thing she could count on was that her mother's need for drugs would outweigh her responsibilities as a parent. Sadly, Mandy learned from a very young age that her mother, Patrice Lewis, was one of those people who could not be trusted.

She realized this truth during her first placement in a foster home with her sisters when she was in grade school. None of them had any idea that most homes had both a mommy and a daddy. Nor did they realize that floors have carpets, that there should be heat in every room of the house, and that most families ate three meals a day. Mr. & Mrs. Hancock were the first couple to introduce Mandy and her sisters to Jesus. They dressed them in itchy dresses and shiny black patent leather shoes that pinched their toes and took them to Sunday school every Sunday.

She never understood what the big fuss was all about regarding the church. She loved the stories about the Jesus man, and the teacher was very kind and gentle, but the other children made her feel uncomfortable. They whispered about her and never wanted to team up with her on projects for fear they'd get cooties, as she overheard one of the boys saying. Once, snooty little Ashley Mulligan told Mandy that she was destined for hell and damnation. She didn't know where this hell and damnation place was, but by the look on snooty Ashley's face, it didn't sound like a place she wanted to go. She didn't really like Sunday school, and she especially didn't like snooty little Ashley Mulligan, but that's where they went every Sunday, anyway. It was what came after the Sunday services, though, that made the itchy crinoline dresses and judgmental eyes of her peers tolerable: lunch in the Hancock kitchen! Momma Hancock was an excellent cook, and every Sunday she made pancakes. The sisters ate them till their tummies felt full to bursting.

Their time at the Hancock's home was wonderful-until Momma made promises to the social workers, and the three girls were, once again, returned to her. Momma hugged and kissed them and made them feel special for several days. The welcome didn't last long, and soon she turned back to drugs and long periods of being gone. Once again, Mandy was left to protect and care for her sisters. Being alone became a regular part of life for the three of them. They would visit one foster home after another when a well-meaning person would notice their mother's absence and report her to officials. Each return from a foster home would merit a move for them as well. *"We'll get a fresh start,"* their momma would promise. Now Mandy understood; she was just trying to relocate and get social services off her trail.

Every time she visited a new foster home, she became more aware of how typical families operate. She often referred to her foster homes as having "*real*" families. "We will have a "*real*" family someday," she vowed to her sisters.

Mandy came to a harsh realization when she was separated from her sisters in high school and placed in a girl's home; her "*real*" family was never going to happen. She was determined to get out of her situation one day and live like the Hancock family and so many others who had welcomed her into their homes. She desired to better herself, and she would never allow anyone to hurt her again. She had taken care of herself for many years, and she could do it for many more. She didn't need anyone else in her life.

Mandy had built her life around mistrust and had always kept up her guard. That's why, in hindsight, she was upset with herself that she had trusted Kade. She had fooled herself into thinking that he would hold her ticket to becoming a real family. When she had been asked to train the new employee, Kade Dean, on that hot, sticky day at the factory over a year ago, she had had no idea that this training with him would change the course of her life forever.

CHAPTER
Five

Ayala smoothed a little extra sunscreen on her shoulders and cheeks. Seeing her reflection in the mirror, she contemplated whether she should dye her hair or not. "So much gray," she exclaimed out loud. Her big brown eyes seemed bigger now with her recent weight loss, and she was pretty sure those wrinkles, which Tim had affectionately called laugh lines, were deeper than before. Still, Ayala Banks had aged gracefully. Stooping to tie her sneakers, she bumped her dresser, causing an item to topple with a thud. She rose to see what she had knocked over and noticed right away what was out of place. The Badge. It was the badge that Tim had worn proudly for forty years. She picked it up, and the weight of it in her hand was oddly comforting. She kept it on her dresser, not only as a reminder of the incredible man who had proudly worn it all those years, but also because it was his policeman status that paved the road to Christ for her.

It was that night thirty-three years ago that a handsome

policeman saved her life and introduced her to the Savior of her soul. Ayala marveled at how she had changed since she met Tim; being married to this man of God had helped her become the woman she was today.

Now and then the enemy of shame crept into her soul, and Ayala would have to remember the promise of Isaiah 54:17 (NKJV):

"No weapon formed against you shall prosper,
And every tongue which rises against you in judgment
You shall condemn.
This is the heritage of the servants of the LORD,
And their righteousness is from Me,"
Says the LORD.

Nothing that the enemy threw at her from her past mattered. She was the Lord's servant, and this was her heritage, which came from Him. She had worked hard at moving forward from her past. Over three decades she'd had Tim by her side to rally and encourage her. He always reminded her she was forgiven and set free and that what the enemy, Satan, had intended for evil God had rewoven for good. She understood that promise with every ounce of her being, but some days when she was caught up in her grief, she became weak and visited those old, dark areas of her life. She relived her past shame from thirty-three years ago, when the sin of promiscuity had caught up with her.

Early on in her life, Ayala had developed a skewed picture of what love was. Offering her body seemed like an excellent way to feel the love she so desperately craved. She didn't understand true love; the kind of love she would later know, by God's grace, with her husband, Tim. An only child born to middle-aged parents, Ayala knew her parents loved her. They were kind parents, but after her father's stroke, in her most impressionable years, her mother seemed to be more focused on caring for him than teaching her inquisitive and lonely teenage daughter the facts of life. Her father's affection was gone. For now, he worked to restore his steps and everything else the stroke had taken from him … except for the relationship he had with his daughter. She was left to care for herself much of the time and found that the arms of a classmate or "this week's boyfriend" comforted her and helped fill the void in her life for the moment. She was well known in high school, but sadly, it wasn't because of her exemplary attitude or academic prowess. Her tainted reputation always went ahead of her. She craved friendships with the popular girls at school—or any girl for that matter. But the only classmates who befriended her were the boys and for the wrong reasons.

Looking back, she realized that she had dodged a bullet many times over. She escaped STDs altogether, which was nothing short of a miracle. She also avoided pregnancy until the winter of 1983. She was shocked when her monthly visitor didn't come around. She had long since moved from her parents' home and even though she took a college class here and there, her focus was on working to support herself and her carefree lifestyle.

She enjoyed her job at the local college coffee shop. She met people from all walks of life, especially college-aged men. She and her roommate often entertained young men in their home overnight. As if this wasn't careless enough, most of the time she didn't even know the young men who shared her bed. Her promiscuity led to an unplanned pregnancy. She had no idea who the father was and didn't want to be bothered with such an inconvenience in her life.

As she stared at the plus mark on the wand before her, which meant she was, in fact, pregnant, she felt there was only one solution for her. Abortion. In Ayala's mind, there were no other choices. She didn't have time for pregnancy and especially didn't have the time or desire for a baby. And with her frivolous lifestyle, being pregnant would cramp her style. Ayala understood that abortion was a controversial subject, especially with the Christian crowd.

Ayala had never stepped foot in a church. She had a few acquaintances growing up who were Christians. She remembered one girl from her class particularly, Stacy Bowles, who was a staunch churchgoer and adamant about the right to life. Stacy went to marches and stood on corners with signs. She remembered thinking

Stacy was a goody-two-shoes type who liked to make a big deal about stuff. Since Ayala didn't go to church, she reasoned that the pro-life views didn't affect her. She never saw abortion as anything other than a quick fix for a predicament that sometimes happens to a woman. It was her body and her choice, after all, wasn't it?

Ayala didn't like to waste time. The morning after she discovered she was pregnant, she called the number to a local abortion clinic her friend had given her. Her friend had used their services on more than one occasion, but after Ayala called and found out the cost of the procedure, she wondered how her friend could afford it even one time.

Ayala cashed out her savings account the next morning. Every cent that she had saved would be used to fix this mistake. Since Ayala's dad had moved to a nursing home and those expenses had drained her parents' account, she knew she couldn't ask them for a loan. She took pride in how she budgeted her money. This financial setback was harder for Ayala to stomach than the actual abortion procedure itself.

She drove to the clinic on the west side of town for her noon appointment. The woman she'd spoken to earlier promised that it wouldn't be painful and she would be in and out of the facility quickly. Not wanting to bother anyone, Ayala chose to drive herself to the clinic in her rusty Buick.

The clinic was old and run down. Paneling seemed to cover every inch of the interior, and the waiting room felt dank and dark. There was a mustiness in the air that combined with the distinct smell of antiseptic to create a nauseating stench. The exam room and procedure room weren't much better. The nurse explained to her how she would have a local anesthetic, and she should feel minimal discomfort throughout the procedure and afterward. She referred to the "termination of the pregnancy" several times. There were many forms to sign, and the nurse asked if she had any questions. Hoping to get this procedure behind her as quickly as possible, she shook her head no and signed the dotted line on the form.

After she urinated in a cup, the nurse confirmed Ayala's

pregnancy with a dip of a strip. She was prepped and wheeled to the surgical area. It seemed to be just a routine part of the day for the assisting staff, and therefore Ayala felt at ease in their care. The little pill they gave her helped take the edge off any nervousness she felt. The cramping she felt during the procedure was bearable, much more so, than the suction noises which caused her to feel nauseous.

When it was over, Ayala felt queasy and crampy, but they told her this would subside. She left with a box of complimentary sanitary pads and instructions on what to do if she experienced any adverse side effects. She glanced at the paper and winced at the thought of having any of the symptoms listed there. She was anxious to go home and get this behind her.

It was difficult for her to get up and walk to the car, and she wished now that she had someone to drive her home. To make matters worse, a group of pro-life supporters had congregated on the sidewalk by the parking lot, and she would have to walk past them to get to her car. The last thing she wanted was a bunch of people trying to make her feel guilty for something she had every right, as an American woman, to do.

One person in the small group carried a sign that said, "Abortion is Murder."

"Murder? Really? Well, that's absurd," Ayala muttered under her breath.

Walking to her car, she heard a woman call out to her, "Jesus will forgive you."

Forgive me for what? Ayala thought as she gingerly got into her car. The signs and remarks angered her. *I haven't done anything illegal! It's my choice, my right*, she thought as she rammed her key into the ignition. The cramping had increased, and Ayala couldn't wait to get home. She started her car and headed out, careful not to make eye contact with anyone. She stopped abruptly at the exit before proceeding and looked left and then right to see if the way was clear.

When she looked right, she saw the full-color posters the pro-life supporters had placed in the grass alongside the sidewalk. They showed the various developments of the growing fetus with pictures depicting what the baby looked like at each stage. It was the very first one that caught her off guard. It read, "Your baby has a heartbeat at five weeks gestation." Her head began to spin, and her queasiness increased. They had determined at the clinic that she was eight weeks along. Was this true? Had she just murdered a baby? *Her* baby?

Ayala sat in her car, staring blankly at the posters. "What have I done?" she cried. "Why didn't anyone tell me?"

CHAPTER Six

Mandy looked forward to her Monday evening ice cream date with her new friend Rae. She had noticed that her passion for ice cream had intensified with her pregnancy. It was undoubtedly one of life's true delicacies for her. But more than her love of ice cream was her love for the girl she had gotten to know over the last couple of months, Rae Carver. Rae was the opposite of Mandy in every way. Rae was from a well-to-do family with a host of people who loved her immensely. Her steady boyfriend had a bright future ahead. Her long unruly auburn hair was always in a mess, which just added to her cuteness. Her green eyes sparkled and danced when she talked; her giggle was infectious. Her character oozed compassion, and you couldn't help but be drawn to her because of her sweet spirit.

In her old way of thinking, Mandy would probably have considered Rae a goody-goody or a Little Miss Perfect. She would have pegged her as a spoiled, squeaky-clean Christian girl. Her lips had probably never muttered a curse word, tasted liquor, or puffed a cigarette. That's how the old Mandy would have viewed her new friend. As part of her recent metamorphosis from sinner to saved person, Mandy was learning to see others through fresh new lenses. She was learning to look at the heart of people, the way Jesus would, instead of judging them by their outward appearance. Having been wronged by so many people in her life, Mandy found this a hard task. It was clear to her, however, that one of Rae's most endearing qualities was that she didn't judge Mandy for how they were different. In Mandy's mind, Rae's heart was as genuine and pure as the most precious of jewels.

Even though her friend Rae was smart, she was indecisive and lacked confidence in many areas. Sometimes, Mandy felt Rae was not so undecided as she was just overly sensitive and caring. She loved her family so much; she was careful not to do or say anything to hurt them—or anyone, for that matter. Despite her indecisiveness, Rae did have some firm convictions that came from a lifetime of loving Jesus, going to church, and growing up in a Christian home. Mandy had learned much from Rae in her new journey as a Christian and could confide in her about anything.

Mandy worried about Rae, though. She would give anything to have such a loving and supportive family as Rae's. Mandy was even jealous of this sometimes. She wished Rae could understand that this kind of love and support were rare and beautiful to someone like herself. Mandy had been trying to convince Rae to talk to her family about all the things going on in her life. For Rae, dodging the issues seemed easier than hurting those she loved, for the time being. She kept telling Mandy that when her boyfriend, Skylar, returned from his study abroad semester in May, they would get everything figured out together. Rae was fortunate to have a guy like Skylar in her life. If Mandy hadn't loved the crazy girl so much, she would be insanely jealous of her!

And she couldn't help but love her. Rae Carver was the best friend Mandy had ever known, even after a short relationship. Mandy and Rae had become roommates through the graciousness of a beautiful Christian woman named Ayala Banks, or Mrs. B, as they affectionately called her.

Mandy still marveled at the way Mrs. B had taken them both into her home. That would never have happened where Mandy came from. She had been brought up not to trust anyone, not even your neighbors. In her neck of the woods, you guarded what was yours with your life. It was utterly unheard of to share your home or your life with someone.

She still couldn't wrap her brain around the way Mrs. B trusted two girls she'd never met. As she became more acquainted with Mrs. B and grew in her relationship with Jesus, she was beginning to understand these strange Christian ways of gentleness, kindness, and compassion. She had a long way to go before she could trust the way Mrs. B or Rae did, but she did know one thing for sure: it felt good to be trusted.

Had Mrs. B not reached out in Christlike compassion and kindness, she would have never known her or Rae. And for this, Mandy was very grateful. She loved the late-night talks she and Rae had been having with Mrs. B lately. She couldn't say where she might be right now without them. Since Mandy had quit her job at the factory early in her pregnancy, money was tight for her. She shuddered to think what might have happened had it not been for the hospitality of Mrs. B

At church, the worship leader would say each Sunday, "God is good," and the congregation replied, "All the time." And then he said again, "All the time," and the congregation responded, "God is good." When she first heard this, she didn't fully understand. On those first Sundays going to church with Mrs. B, there was a lot that didn't make sense. She wondered how anyone in her situation could think God was good all the time. But slowly, it was sinking in for Mandy. She was starting to understand God's goodness and provision for her. Her living situation was an excellent example of this. In the hardest time of her life, God had provided two of the most caring and giving people in the world to walk alongside her. Not only had they ministered to her through meeting her basic needs, but her spiritual needs—which she didn't even know she was lacking—were also being met.

These two women were teaching her how to see life according to the scriptures. In the past, Mandy would most likely have shrugged off the events of the past few months as coincidence. She probably wouldn't even have recognized Mrs. B and Rae as true friends. But through the grace of Jesus, the scales of bitterness and mistrust were slowly falling away from Mandy's eyes, and she was able to see more clearly that "God is good—all the time."

The phone in her pocket jingled, and she picked it up to look at the text. She snickered to herself when she saw Rae was running late—and not surprised that her friend said she couldn't decide what to wear. She texted back that Rae had better hurry, or else she might order for both and eat it all.

While she waited for her friend, Mandy was entertained by the toddler in the corner with the bouncy, blonde curls. She was a girl after Mandy's own heart as she hung her mouth open for more ice cream before her mother could even get another bite onto the spoon. She was darling, and Mandy was amused to see how the momma would open her mouth also when the little girl took a bite. Pretty soon Momma made an "all gone" gesture with her hands and said, "All gone Olivia, it's all gone!" Little Olivia looked mighty disappointed that the creamy deliciousness was over, but the toy Momma pulled out of the bag seemed to make things all right in her world again.

Mandy quietly formed the name on her lips: "Olivia." She liked the sound of the little girl's name. She hadn't yet given much thought to what she would call the little one growing in her tummy. She'd been so busy just trying to survive from day to day and planning for her little ones' future that she hadn't thought about a name for her. Olivia would be on the list of baby names to consider.

The thought of naming her baby sent her into a bit of a panic. Names were important. They needed to be unique. She liked it when names were chosen to honor someone or when a name had special meaning. Like Mrs. B's name for instance. Mandy about fell over the day Mrs. B told her what her name, Ayala, meant. It was the day she met her, the day she and her baby were rescued on the steps of the abortion clinic. In fact, learning the meaning of her name was the moment when Mandy knew she could trust Ayala Banks.

Mandy was already apprehensive on that day she went to the abortion clinic. She had just endured several discouraging days after learning she was pregnant and her life seemed to be spiraling out of control. She loved Kade, and she thought he felt the same; after all, he said he did. But Mandy found out; his love for her was only as good as the five hundred dollars he had given her toward an abortion. She was shocked at how Kade responded when she told him the news of the baby. He let her know, without hesitation, that he wasn't ready to settle down and have a kid, but he'd be happy to give her some money to go toward "taking care of it." Mandy took his money because she certainly couldn't "take care of it" by herself, but that was the last thing she'd ever take from Kade Dean. She would wash her hands of him once and for all. No one would hurt her again like this.

Mandy knew she couldn't stomach going back to the factory and facing him every day, so she put in her notice. Without the job, she'd have to find another, which put her at risk of losing her apartment. Her apartment was just a small place, and although the rent was reasonable, she still barely made ends meet. Alone, facing unemployment, and having no support system, Mandy decided that an abortion was the best solution for her situation. Having quit her job at the factory, she no longer saw Kade, and he had made it clear, through his lack of communication, that the relationship was over. He hadn't texted or called her since he handed her the cash and the curt response to their dilemma. He didn't even offer to drive her to the appointment, to hold her hand or anything.

She decided to look for work after the abortion. Her body would need a few days to recover from the procedure, while her heart would need a lifetime to heal from the heartbreak Kade had caused her. She mustered up the strength on a chilly October morning to get to the abortion clinic by herself. The clinic wasn't too far from her apartment. She was relieved about this since her old car wasn't very reliable. She just hoped it would get her there and back without breaking down, as it had the habit of doing lately. She had driven past the clinic many times over the years. It was easy to spot, as there was typically a group of pro-life demonstrators gathered close to the entrance. She was always amazed at how devoted the pro-life people were. They were out there with their signs supporting the right to life, rain or shine.

On that day, as she saw them gathered between her and the door, she wondered if those people understood women like her—women who had nothing...no money, no family, no support...no baby daddy. Didn't they know that for some women ... abortion was the only choice that made sense? But even though that was her thinking now, Mandy couldn't silence conflicting thoughts. She remembered back in the day when she went to Sunday school with the Hancock family and all the stories about the God of love and how He had created each person in His image. She never fully understood what that meant, but her teacher made it clear that every life had a purpose.

Mandy didn't know how far along she was in her pregnancy, and she was confused about whether it was considered a baby at this point. When she called for the appointment, the woman she spoke to never used the word *baby*; she just used the word *pregnancy*. She used phrases like *when the pregnancy is terminated* or *when you are free from the pregnancy*. The counselor never used the word *baby*, so Mandy was uncertain how to feel about it. All she understood was that a pregnancy eventually turns into a baby, and she could not handle either, in any way.

She settled on having the abortion but was still apprehensive. Perhaps it was because of a recurring forest dream she was having. On the night before her appointment, she had the dream again, but this time there was more detail. Most nights she got to a specific part of the vision and would wake up never knowing what happened. The dream would linger and stay with her. She could remember all the details of it the next day. It wasn't fuzzy or pieced together as some dreams are. This dream was different, like a real adventure or a television series that got flipped on with a switch as soon as she fell asleep. It happened consecutively, two or three nights in a row. But on the night before her scheduled procedure, her dream continued. It so disturbed Mandy that she awoke the next morning with second thoughts about her abortion. Confused and wondering if she was making the right decision, Mandy kept her appointment anyway.

CHAPTER
Seven

Rae left Dean Wilson's office with fresh new tears rolling down her face. She had cried a lot of tears of failure over the last few months, but this time she cried tears of failure in academics. When the e-mail from the dean arrived, asking her to come to his office, she had a feeling why he wanted to see her, and she was right. Her GPA was slipping, and her scholarship money would slip with it if she didn't pick up the pace in her classes soon.

With a sense of panic rising in her chest, she slipped into the women's restroom and took a seat in the stall, buried her head in her hands, and sobbed. She so wished she could talk to Skylar. She had tried private messaging him but had not received a response. She knew when he left on his study-abroad trip to Cambodia that communication would be infrequent if at all. He told her how he would be "roughing it" with his study group in the Cambodian mountains, camping and living off the grid and learning as much about the Cambodian culture as he could. She understood the trip was an invaluable experience for him and influential in his field of study in social sciences, but she selfishly wished him back.

He was so excited about going, and she couldn't wait to hear all about his adventures. The last time she had seen him was over the Thanksgiving holiday. It felt like an eternity had passed, as if he had just fallen off the face of the earth. She craved time with him. She had known Skylar Weaver since they shared Cheerios with each other in the church nursery. They grew up going to Sunday school and church camp together. They were even baptized at the same time at Willow Pond. She had already married Skylar Weaver, more than once, when they were preschoolers. Left to entertain themselves in the playroom, during the Bible study her mom hosted in their home, a pretend wedding would often break out with the other children in attendance. She was always the bride, Skylar was the groom, and her best friend Sadie was usually the preacher. Rae wore high heels and a long head scarf, which she retrieved from the dress up box. Skylar wore a tie, and they turned the toy box upside down for Pastor Sadie to marry them while holding a Dr. Seuss "Bible" in her hand! She loved Skylar Weaver back then, and she would forever love him.

Skylar loved Jesus more than he loved Rae, and that was what she loved most about him. He was a pure gentleman, and he and Rae had sworn they would remain sexually pure until they were married. They had remained firm in their vow of abstinence, until Thanksgiving break. They were alone at his parents' home, realizing that they wouldn't see each other again for six months and caught up in the heat of the moment. On that day Rae and Skylar broke their vows of purity. Afterward, they were both ashamed of what had happened and swore it would never happen again. They spent time in prayer together, asking God to forgive them and for the strength to recommit to their vows of purity. Before Skylar left, they both felt content in their relationship with each other and with God. However, Rae was unsure how she'd make it that long without talking to him. Other than seeing the occasional pictures and updates posted on the Study Abroad Facebook page about the trip and catching a glimpse of him looking tanned and tired at a Cambodian campsite; she had not had contact with him since before he left over Christmas break.

In January, when Rae's monthly period didn't come for the second time, she feared she might be pregnant. A pregnancy test confirmed her fears, and life after that became one downhill battle after another. Her morning sickness was so intense that she missed a lot of her classes; in turn, her grades began to fall. At the beginning of the semester, she had begged her parents to let her stay off campus and live in an apartment with friends. Her parents had agreed if she would use her part-time job to help pay the rent. She couldn't keep up with her job because she was trying to make up for time missed in class, and so her roommates gave her a two-week notice to find another living arrangement.

With her background in pharmaceuticals, Rae knew enough about pregnancy to realize she needed to get started on prenatal vitamins. A friend had told her about a Christian pregnancy resource center called the Center for Hope. The center did free testing, gave out free vitamins, and offered pregnancy and parenting classes. With no money of her own to see a doctor, she visited the center and met Ayala Banks, also known as Mrs. B, who counseled with her each week. Mrs. B helped her get the vitamins and information she needed, along with much-needed encouragement and prayer support.

Rae found a confidante in Mrs. B and, through many tears, explained her situation to her. When Mrs. B learned that Rae risked losing her current living arrangement, she graciously offered her a room in her home until she got some things figured out. The Center for Hope, and especially Mrs. B, became the lifeline Rae clung to during this storm in her life. What a blessing Mrs. B was in her life! Rae didn't know what she would have done without her. Not only was she able to stay there and glean wisdom from this incredibly generous woman, but she also had the awesome opportunity to walk alongside her new friend, Mandy, who had just accepted Jesus as her Savior. Rae loved having a front-row seat to watch Mandy's life unfold as she now walked, hand in hand, with Jesus in her journey.

The time Rae spent with Mandy and Mrs. B in Bible study and prayer was one of the few things that had gotten her through these last difficult months.

Even though Rae was overwhelmed by her circumstances, she was reminded daily of what a mighty God she served and how He brought people into her life when she needed them the most. Rae was keenly aware now more than ever that when she was weak, Jesus was strong! Rae relied heavily on Jesus right now. He was her hope, and she trusted He would give her wisdom in the days ahead. It was hard to always keep her eyes on Him though, especially on days like today when she had to jump over one more hurdle until she could talk to Skylar and they could figure some things out together. Overwhelmed and guilt-ridden, Rae felt as if she was forever back-paddling in a boat going nowhere.

One thing that she had learned from her new friend Mandy was to take one day at a time, one task at a time. Mandy was the strongest person she had ever met. She couldn't imagine what all she had been through in her life. Even though she and Mandy had led different lives and were opposite of each other in many ways, they had one major thing in common. Rae and Mandy both loved their babies and wanted only the best for them. There was a minor commonality they also shared: their love for ice cream. It was a passion, indeed. And to combine the two commonalities was pure bliss.

Just last night, on their weekly ice cream date, Mandy shared how she had found strength and hope in a Bible verse she read that day. "But he said to me, 'My grace is sufficient for you, for my power is made perfect in weakness.' Therefore, I will boast all the more gladly about my weaknesses, so that Christ's power may rest on me" (2 Corinthians 12:9 NIV). This verse couldn't have been timelier for Rae and she decided to claim it for herself this day also.

Rae blew her nose and spent some time in prayer in the stall. She prayed for wisdom and strength, but most of all, she prayed she would remember that His grace was sufficient for all her needs.

CHAPTER
Eight

Ayala was extra tired today. She hadn't slept well the last few weeks. She couldn't pinpoint why. Perhaps it was the hope of spring in the air. She loved to garden, and the unusually warm late April days had brought plants and shrubs into bloom earlier than usual this year. It felt like spring in Indiana, but she had lived there long enough to know that cold winds would blow again, and she didn't want to plant until she was sure the threat of frost was over. With some extra mouths to feed in her home, fresh vegetables would be welcome, and she had put a lot of thought into what to plant.

She had picked up gardening once again, the spring after Tim died, for therapy mostly. For two years when he was sick, she put all her time into caring for him and making memories while they could. When Tim was in good health, they enjoyed gardening together and were proud salsa makers. Tim knew all the different kinds of hot peppers and tried his green thumb and taste buds on most of them. Tim loved to try new things and dabbled in various hobbies after he retired from the police force. Her late husband was a fearless adventure seeker and exhibited this character in his faith as well. He had no fear in sharing Jesus with others, no matter who they were or where they were. To Tim, planting Jesus seeds was the best kind of gardening there was.

He certainly hadn't had any fear that night when he approached her on the bridge, thirty-three years ago. In the days and weeks that followed Ayala's abortion, she couldn't rest. She had haunting nightmares of babies crying or of having blood on her hands. When she'd close her eyes at night, all she could see was the sign the pro-life supporters carried that said, "Abortion is murder." She spent hours in the library looking up information on abortion and even went back to the clinic and picked up a few of the pamphlets that the pro-life advocates were handing out. The pro-life brochures did not match the information she had received inside the building on the day of her procedure. The more research she did on her own, the more Ayala was convinced that she had made a terrible mistake. There was no getting around it: she had taken a human life. This harsh reality gnawed at her soul day and night, and she became physically ill over who she had become. She felt selfish, insensitive, and callous. Ayala hated the person she had created herself to be through her lifestyle choices over the last several years. Her quest for a good time, to find momentary satisfaction, had cost a life: her own child's life.

These thoughts and feelings consumed Ayala. She became engulfed by a deep, dark depression that grabbed her like a thief in the night and plunged her into an endless abyss of despair. She stayed home in bed instead of going to work. These feelings consumed her thoughts, and she felt as if she was living in a fog. Her absences at work resulted in the loss of her job. Soon to follow was the loss of self-esteem and eventually the will to live. As her situation grew darker and more desperate, Ayala decided that the world would be better off if she no longer contributed to it. In Ayala's depressed and confused state, she concluded that the only way to make up for taking her child's life was to take her own.

She made her decision, and late one cold winter's night, Ayala drove her car to Jackson Bridge, planning to take a plunge into the icy waters below. In her mind, it seemed a fitting death for such an ice-cold killer. She walked alongside the bridge walkway. She stood for a moment and then climbed to the top rung of the three-tiered railing and sat down. She could feel the cold metal through her blue jeans. Her bare hands stuck to the rafters, and the frigid wind took her breath. These conditions, however, paled in comparison to the icy blood she felt running through her veins. She felt as if nothing warm was left in her soul. She was determined to take the plunge. Now that she was up on top, she just had to work up the nerve.

While making his late-night rounds, Officer Tim Banks saw the silhouette of a person sitting on the top railing of Jackson Bridge. A freezing night, the late hour, feet dangling over the side … Officer Banks surmised this was a disaster waiting to happen.

He parked his car and walked toward the figure. Getting closer to the bridge; he could see it was a woman who sat there shivering. "Ma'am, I'm Officer Banks. Kind of a cold night to be sitting on the bridge, isn't it?" he asked.

Startled, Ayala threw a glance down his way and shouted, "I'm not doing anything wrong. You don't need to be concerned."

"It is my concern when someone is in danger, ma'am, and it appears to me that you are in danger up there," Tim replied as he walked closer, hoping he'd be able to grab her if she decided to take the plunge.

"I'm fine—go away!"

"Well, ma'am, I'm not the smartest guy around, but taking all the factors here into consideration, I'm guessing you're not fine. What do you say I help you down and you let me know what's going on? Maybe I can help or find someone to help you."

"No, please, leave me alone. I don't need your help or anyone else's help. I know what I need to do: I'm doing what I deserve!" Her voice was shaky with cold and fear.

Tim could see that the woman before him was gripping the railing tightly, and he doubted whether she would follow through, but all the same, he wanted to get her down from the railing as quickly as possible. It was in life-or-death situations such as these in his job that he wasn't afraid to witness for Christ. People who were at this point in their lives needed a Savior and the hope that came from Him. That was Tim's approach on this night.

"Well, ma'am, I don't know what brought you to this point, but I believe we all have a purpose in life." Tim continued, "I believe we were all created uniquely with a plan in mind. Nothing we do can keep us from the love of the one who created us. There is forgiveness available to us, and from that forgiveness comes peace."

The woman had grown quiet, and he could tell she was listening, so he continued. "Look, I don't know what's going on in your life, but I do know you are loved and valued, and there is hope and healing for you. Please let me help you down, and I'd love to share more about that with you." He wanted to shimmy up the banister and throw her on his back, but he feared any sudden moves would make her jump. She was going to need gentle coaxing. He breathed a quick and silent prayer asking God to soften her heart to his words and give him the wisdom to do what he needed to do to get her down.

She remained quiet but shifted her weight a little as if she was antsy. Officer Banks was getting ready to speak when she snapped back at him, "I assume you're talking about Jesus. Jesus is the one who will forgive me? Well, I've heard that before—but will He forgive a murderer?"

Baffled by what he was hearing, Tim wondered what he might be up against. Was he dealing with a murderer? There hadn't been any calls about a murder or a domestic dispute or anything during his night rounds. If there was a victim somewhere who needed help, he needed to find out.

"Ma'am, are you saying that you're a murderer? Do I need to send help somewhere? Please tell me what's going on, so I can get help to someone if they need it."

"Yes, I am! I murdered my baby!" she sobbed. He could see her body shaking with emotion and hoped she would keep her grip on the railing. He was sickened to hear that she had killed her child. In his job, he had heard stories of women with postpartum depression who had killed their babies. He wondered if this might be the case.

"Ma'am, can you tell me where your baby is now? Please let me help you down so we can get this figured out." He began to take slow steps toward the bottom of the railing.

"My baby is dead; I killed it. I had no idea it had a heartbeat … I didn't even know it was really a baby!" she confessed through her tormented sobs.

Officer Banks pulled his coat tighter around his neck. He was trying desperately to make sense of what he was hearing. "My name is Tim, by the way. Mind if I ask your name?"

"Ayala." Her tone was quick and harsh.

"Well, Ayala, when did you give birth to your baby?"

Ayala's broken heart sank into the pit of her stomach. "That's just it," she sobbed. "I didn't give birth to my baby. I killed it before it even had a chance to live!"

By now her body was heaving from the weight of what she'd done, and Officer Banks feared that she would lose what little balance she had on the railing and fall to her death for sure. He was quickly putting together all the bits and pieces he was gathering and trying to come up with a plan. Apparently, this young woman had had an abortion, and the decision had tormented her to the point of suicide.

It was all coming clear to him now. He knew he had to get up there and somehow bring her down. He called up to her, "Oh, I see. Ayala, did you have an abortion?"

She managed to mutter an "Uh-huh" through her sobs.

"Listen," he continued, "I can't imagine what you're going through, but I do believe that every person has a soul, even the unborn. And I believe with all my heart that your baby is in heaven in the loving arms of Jesus. Ayala, you can meet your baby someday, and I'd like to tell you how. Let me come help you down."

The freezing conditions only intensified Ayala's confusion, and she felt that her mind was twirling out of control. The thought of jumping into her icy grave below was terrifying. She didn't know what to think anymore. Could it be true what the officer was saying? After all, what the Christian pro-life supporters were saying was true; she had learned that from her research.

She was paralyzed with fear and gripped the railing tightly. Through uncontrollable sobs, she managed to blurt out to the officer below, "I'm so scared!"

Officer Banks called out that he was going to climb to her and help her down. She was losing her resolve; he knew there was no more asking or pleading or trying to convince her. He was going to have to go up and get her.

Tim began the climb up to the third railing where she was. He assured her she would be okay and encouraged her to hang on tightly. The courageous officer anchored himself by putting one leg outside the second railing so that the third rung would provide support for him. He put his arm around her middle and gently coaxed her to swing her legs to the other side while hanging on to the supports with her hands.

The officer's strong arms were comforting to Ayala. Her fear started to subside, and she put her focus on his words and getting down. Finally, with his help, she was on the other side of the railing, and the two of them climbed down slowly. Ayala's unprotected fingers were numb now, and her feet were just as frozen. Officer Banks led her to his cruiser and helped her into the backseat. Then he pulled a blanket from his trunk and covered her with it.

He slid behind the wheel and shut the door. He shot a prayer of thanksgiving heavenward because he knew it was only through God's strength that he had managed to help Ayala down from that bridge. He took a deep breath and pulled into traffic toward Mercy Hospital.

CHAPTER Nine

Rae and Mandy sipped their drive-through milk-shakes as they drove to the Center for Hope together. They loved it when they could go to their appointments at the same time. The Center for Hope had helped them both make many important decisions. The counselors educated them on their growing babies and changing bodies. The young women would also learn about the stages of labor and how to care for their newborns as they progressed. The staff was especially instrumental in assisting Mandy in her newfound journey with Jesus.

Mostly, Mandy enjoyed the atmosphere of the center and the sense of peace and calm she sensed while there. Mrs. B said this was the presence of the Holy Spirit, and even though Mandy didn't fully understand who the Holy Spirit was, she believed God's presence must surely be there at the center. Mandy felt His presence in the love and compassion shown to her. She never felt judged or insignificant. Having Rae ride along with her just magnified the joy in the experience. Rae could always make her smile.

Today, however, Rae wasn't her bubbly self, and Mandy could tell she was troubled. "So, I have an idea. How about we make a side trip to the Baby Department Store after our appointments?" Mandy suggested. "You know, just to browse and dream a little?" She hoped to provide a pleasant diversion for her stressed friend.

Rae managed a half smile. "I don't think so tonight, Mandy. I really need to study. I just found out that if I don't get my grades up at the end of the semester, I'm going to lose my scholarship. That will really make my dad curious … and furious."

Mandy's eyes drifted from the road briefly, and she glanced at her friend. "Rae, your parents sound so sweet. You're lucky to have them in your life, you know? Why don't you just be honest with them and tell them about the baby? They may be upset at first, but I have a feeling, if they're half the people you say they are, they will come around to the idea eventually, and everything will work out. I'm so worried the stress of all of this is just going to make matters worse for you."

"Oh, Mandy," Rae sighed, "it's much more complicated than that. I really want to tell Skylar before I tell anyone else. I want him by my side when I tell my parents. I know how Skylar operates! Believe me, all of this will be much harder on him if he finds out I had to bear the burden of telling my parents on my own. He'll never forgive himself. He will want to share in the responsibility of breaking this news to our parents.

"Skylar Weaver is a man of integrity, and I know he will feel as though he's let me down when he finds out. If I go ahead and tell our parents, I'm afraid he'll feel like he's let them down by not being the man he claims to be. We made this baby together, and we need to be together when we tell our parents. It will be the best for everyone, I promise. He will agree."

"I need his support, Mandy. I need to have him beside me." She straightened in her seat and fixed her gaze on the road. "I just have to hang in there until he is home, no matter what!" Trying to escape the weight of the moment before she burst into tears again, Rae cleared her throat as if to shift gears. "I mean, I only have to wait …

twenty days, eight hours, and twenty-five minutes, to be exact—but who's counting?"

Mandy could see that she wanted to change the subject and move on. She could also understand why Rae would want to have Skylar beside her. She fully understood the importance of having his support. Even though she often wished things might have played out differently with Kade, she realized now that it wasn't meant to be.

Even though Kade was absent from her life now, she thought of him every time she saw her ever-changing reflection in the mirror. Her mind often returned to that hot sticky day at the factory when she was training him and how special he made her feel. She fell quickly for his sense of humor and the way he teased her about driving the forklift in the warehouse. She remembered with fondness how he stood in the bucket of the cherry picker they used to pull things from the top shelves and called out to her with a corny Romeo impression, asking her out on their first date. He had tried several times to ask her out, but she always turned him down. However, his Romeo impression was so over the top, she couldn't resist.

She daydreamed quite a bit about their first date at the county fair, complete with a romantic Ferris wheel ride and a shared cone of cotton candy. Every outing with Kade was an adventure. He always made things fun and exciting. Even a trip to the local thrift shop to pick up T-shirts was filled with laughter as he tried on clunky shoes and old hats and played a game of "Guess who I am?" with her.

Mandy missed Kade. She missed his phone calls, his silly text messages with heart symbols and smiley faces. Most of all, she missed the feeling of being in love, even though she now knew the feeling was not mutual. Had it been, Kade would have supported his child, the child they created together.

Thinking of him always reminded her of what a fool she'd been to trust him and believe that he loved her. Despite her heartbreak and disappointment, Mandy now realized that things had turned out the way they had with Kade for a reason.

After all, if Kade had accompanied her to the abortion clinic that day, she would not know Rae or Mrs. B or this little sweetie growing in her tummy. But most important, Mandy would not know Jesus. At last, she had found true love in her Savior—the unconditional love that never dies and is ever forgiving, the kind of love she had never known before.

One night, during their prayer time, Mrs. B had prayed that God would send Mandy a man someday who would love her the way Christ loves His church. Mandy asked Mrs. B later what that meant. Mrs. B explained that the church is God's people. God created His people, and nothing can separate them from His love. Mrs. B was praying that God would send a man to Mandy who would love her this passionately. Mandy liked this prayer. She was learning from Mrs. B how to pray. She desired to experience this type of love, the kind of love she had witnessed in her foster parents over the years, the type of love Rae had for Skylar. She wanted to be able to talk about the love she shared with her husband, even if she grieved him, as Mrs. B so affectionately spoke about Mr. Banks.

She loved Mrs. B's story. She had encouraged her many times to write it down and make it into a romance novel. It was sure to be a best seller. Mr. Banks had been Mrs. B's rescuer. He had rescued her from the bridge the night she wanted to kill herself after her abortion. He had promised to tell her how she could see her baby again, and after Mrs. B spent a couple of days in the hospital, he visited her and made good on that promise. That was the day he led Mrs. B to Jesus. That was the day she was forgiven and set free from the darkness that had engulfed her for so long. She started going to a Bible study and services at his church. There she fell more in love with Jesus and more in love with the man who had introduced them, Officer Tim Banks.

Mandy wanted a storybook love like the one Mr. and Mrs. Banks had. Their love for Jesus and each other ran deep, and Mrs. B continued to keep his legacy alive by doing meaningful work, just as she had promised Tim she would before he died. Mandy was thankful to have benefited by such action. Mrs. B was determined to pay forward the blessing Mr. Banks had brought her many years before, and now she had become Mandy's rescuer. When Mandy would tease Mrs. B about being her rescuer, she would reply, "Oh, Mandy. I'm not your rescuer. I was just the tool to get the job done!"

Undoubtedly, God had used Ayala Banks to rescue her on the steps of the abortion clinic. She was desperately in need of rescue that day, as she was already apprehensive after a restless night. That night, Mandy dreamed of being in the woods again, frightened, confused, and following the doe to whom she felt strangely connected.

The doe led Mandy to a circular rock pile, and when she looked in, she saw the source of the doe's angst. Apparently, this rock pile was meant to serve as a barrier or a warning by a fisherman or someone who had visited the river, because inside the circle was a sinkhole. The hole was several feet down, and at the bottom of the hole, Mandy could see white spots. There in the darkness of the pit were the telltale markings of a tiny fawn. Clearly the doe now pacing frantically around the rocks, panting and softly grunting, was its mother.

Mandy didn't know if the young deer was alive or not, but she could see how desperate the doe was to have her baby rescued from the dark hole. Mandy knew she had to save the little fawn. She was impressed by the doe's sacrifices made for her baby. This doe had put herself in harm's way; she had approached a human and trusted her. Mandy couldn't back away now. She respected her determination and devotion despite the odds. Even when she was dreaming, Mandy's survival skills kicked in.

As she sized up the situation, she realized that the hole was too deep for her to reach in and lift the baby out. She would need a tool of some sort, but she had limited resources. How would she pull the little guy out, and was she dealing with a live animal or a dead animal?

Mandy had no idea what she was going to do, but she knew with every ounce of her being that she had to rescue the fawn.

CHAPTER Ten

Rae watched the video entitled *Your Developing Baby* at the Center for Hope. She was intrigued by it all. She marveled at how God had knit her baby together in her womb. Undoubtedly, he or she was fearfully and wonderfully made in God's image, as scripture said. Pregnancy should be one of the happiest times of her life; carrying the baby of the man she loved. Rae had dreamt of it ever since she and Skylar were in junior high. She dreamt of spending her life with him and raising a family together. But here she was, having his baby, and he didn't even know about it. As for happy—well, she wasn't necessarily feeling that too much these days either.

Once again Rae had failed to silence her phone, and during the film, she heard the ding of her private message ringtone from her purse. She gave a glance to her counselor, who was watching the video with her, and mouthed the word *sorry*. Her mind now wandering from the video, she wondered if her study group was messaging her about their upcoming assignment. It was a big assignment due in just a few days, and Rae had not even begun doing the research. She shook it off and tried to focus on the video, knowing the counselor would want to discuss it afterward. It was challenging for her to concentrate on just one thing these days; there were too many things demanding her attention.

Mandy was waiting for Rae in the lobby when the class was over, and they headed out into the rain. They giggled all the way to the car, clomping through the puddles with their backpacks over their heads against the spring shower. Mandy was thankful Mrs. B had loaned them her vehicle, since hers had recently been towed to the junkyard, and Rae didn't use hers much because she couldn't afford the gas.

"Did you have a good meeting?" Mandy asked as she adjusted the steering wheel to accommodate her bulging middle.

"Yes, we watched a video on the developing baby. It was amazing to see. I can't wait to get my ultrasound and have a look at my baby!"

"Are you going to find out the gender of the baby?" Mandy asked.

"I don't know. I guess I'll wait and see what Skylar wants to do. However, I think it would be kind of fun to wait and see in the delivery room." Then the indecisive side of Rae kicked in. "Still, knowing whether it's a boy or a girl would be good for planning. Oh my, more decisions! Aaack!" she exclaimed whirling her hands on either side of her head.

Mandy giggled. "And I suppose you will name this baby Skylar Jr. or Rae Jr.?"

"Wait!" Rae smirked, "You mean I have to name this kid too? Well, then Junior it will be!" Rae's eyes twinkled. "Whew, I'm glad that's settled. At least that's one less thing I have to figure out!"

Mandy laughed out loud at her friend's comical words. "Wow, I sure hope this kid is a boy! A girl named Junior might get made fun of!"

It was good to share a laugh with Rae. Knowing how stressed she had been lately, Mandy asked if there was anything she could do to help her once they got home.

"Yeah, sure," Rae said with excitement. "You can do my research, get with my study group, chart the evidence, and then write my paper for me if you want!" This statement jogged Rae's memory, and she thought about the private message that had arrived during her video lesson. She began to dig around in her backpack frantically. "Oh, that reminds me, I need to check my messages 'cause I heard it ding at the meeting."

She kept talking while searching. "You know, I have this study group that is so diverse. There's me, who is just terrible at putting things off to the last minute right now, a guy who doesn't seem to do anything, and then this other girl who is an overachiever. I mean, she would probably just do the whole project for us if I gave her the go-ahead." She finally retrieved her phone from the bottom of her backpack and poked in the passcode. "And actually, I'm considering—" Rae stopped in mid-sentence. "Oh no!" she exclaimed.

Mandy could see that Rae was looking at her phone with her free hand to her mouth and shock in her eyes. "What's wrong, Rae?"

"This private message," Rae sputtered. "It's from Skylar—I missed my opportunity to chat with him!"

Mandy sensed her disappointment. "What? You've got to be kidding, Rae. What did he say?"

Rae grazed her finger over the screen and read the message out loud to Mandy.

Rae, I just have a few minutes of computer time and am unable to access my email.

I got your message, and I am in total shock. I'm trying to process all of this.

I'll be home in 2-½ weeks, and we can talk about it then. In the meantime,

I'll be praying about all this and ask God to help us.

I agree that we need to tell our parents together. I don't want you having to face them by yourself.

I'm sorry you've had to go through this alone.

I love you and will call you as soon as I can.

And that was it. Now Skylar knew about their baby. Rae had such conflicting thoughts. She wondered if she had done the wrong thing by telling him via private message. She feared this would ruin the next two weeks of his trip. When she sent the initial message, she wavered about what she should say. If she emphasized the urgency to talk to him, he might worry. Therefore, she opted just to go ahead and tell him that she was pregnant, scared, confused, and waiting for him to talk to their parents. Now she worried if she should have told him at all. But then, what a surprise he'd have when he saw her for the first time, pregnant belly and all, when he returned. Most of all, she just wanted him to know. She needed someone close to her to understand, someone who would tell her what to do.

Two and a half weeks until she would see Skylar and they could figure out the rest of their lives together. Two and a half weeks; Rae hoped she could wait. She missed him so much it hurt. She longed for him to hold her close and tell her it would all be okay, just like he'd done when her brother Kurt was injured in a car accident four years ago. They almost lost Kurt. They did lose Kurt, in a sense. The brain damage he suffered had taken away the fun-loving brother who teased her and played pranks on her as they grew up.

When they got the phone call about Kurt's accident and learned that he most likely wouldn't survive the night, it was Skylar who stood by her every step of the way. He and Kurt were friends; still were. Kurt had to learn almost everything over again, and even though he had mastered walking and most motor skills, his cognitive skills were lacking. Her sweet brother was like a little boy most of the time now. It was disheartening for the family to see Kurt this way, but they were thankful to have him. His survival alone was a miracle. His rehab would not have gone so well if it had not been for the steady hand, the strong back and the godly encouragement of Skylar, which saw Kurt through some tough times.

At Thanksgiving, when they last saw Skylar, Kurt, in his childlike state, cried and clung to him. You would have thought Skylar was leaving for years, the way Kurt carried on. That was how Rae wanted to carry on right now. She understood Kurt's grief. The thought of throwing a tantrum tempted her. If it would get her closer to seeing Skylar, she would. She missed him that much. Two and a half weeks—she wasn't sure if she could make it.

CHAPTER
Eleven

"Mandy Lewis?" Mandy stood up and smoothed her shirt over her baby bump as she walked toward the woman in the doorway. Uncertainties about the upcoming meeting made her a bit shaky, and she hoped her nervousness wasn't noticeable.

A woman at the Center for Hope had recommended she see Beth Tudor. Beth called herself a life coach. She specialized in helping women in crisis pregnancy situations make decisions regarding their future. She was a pro-life supporter and a Christian, so Mandy felt good about talking to her.

She had been dealing with a lot of anguish and confusion over her future and the future of her baby. She had shared some of her hopes, dreams, and fears with one of the counselors at the Center for Hope. The counselor referred her to Beth. She had sent other girls to Beth who were in situations like Mandy's, with success. Sorting out her thoughts and feelings with a professional sounded like a good idea to Mandy, and she agreed to a meeting.

She was led to a small office and asked to wait. It wasn't posh or extravagant but quaint and orderly. There wasn't a lot of decoration in the room except for a portrait of what Mandy assumed was Beth Tudor's family. It was a lovely photo, framed in a big, elegant frame. Mandy got lost in the happiness of the family photo. Beth and her husband sat on a blanket stretched out upon a well-manicured lawn with a brick house in the background. They each held a child on their lap and were flanked by a child on either side. There was a child in the middle as well. Wow, five kids! Mandy marveled at the thought of having five children.

But the thing that struck her most about the photograph was that three of the children had the distinct features of Beth and her husband: fair skin and blond hair, with the youngest girl almost the spitting image of Beth herself. But two of the children were dark-skinned. Two darling little girls who had spiky ponytails poking all around their heads with bright, broad smiles. Beth and her husband apparently had adopted children. Mandy's heart was warmed at seeing the family photo of all those beautiful children. Even though they didn't all look alike, they looked like they belonged together. They looked like a family—a big, happy one at that.

Surrounding the photo were framed degrees, with the name Elizabeth Wilson on the first one from a law school out east. The second one, inscribed to Elizabeth Wilson Tudor in fancy writing, stated she had a bachelor's degree in social work. *Wow, this Beth Tudor is one ambitious woman,* she mused. She couldn't imagine what it would be like to work so hard and raise a house full of kids at the same time.

Soon the woman in the portrait entered the room, looking every bit as charming as she did in the photo. She stuck her hand out. "Good morning, Mandy; I'm Beth Tudor. So glad to meet you!"

As Mandy shook her hand, Beth made eye contact with her, and she noticed that she was quite pretty. With straight white teeth and a gleam in her eye, Beth had a natural beauty about her.

"Can I get a drink for you, water, hot tea or something?" She smiled at Mandy as she poured herself a glass of water from the sidebar.

"No, thank you." Mandy grinned. "I'd be running for the little girl's room pretty soon if I did," she said with a gesture toward her belly.

Beth laughed. "Oh yes, I remember those days well. It's just amazing how everything gets pushed and shoved around to make room for baby, isn't it?" Mandy nodded in agreement.

They spent some time chitchatting about the rigors of pregnancy, the weather, and some of the services Beth offered. Beth was sensitive to Mandy's apparent nervousness and waited until she felt comfortable before beginning to ask her questions. She wanted to build a relationship with Mandy, as she understood she needed to gain her trust with such a delicate subject.

Soon Beth started to ask some questions. "Mandy, what would be your idea of a perfect life for your baby?"

Mandy told her about the foster homes she had been in as a child and how she longed to have a real family her whole life. "I guess a perfect life would mean she'd be in a safe place where she can grow without fear."

She spoke from her own experiences and desires when she mentioned that a child should be nurtured, disciplined with love, and supported emotionally and financially. "Oh, and yes, of course, to be taught about Jesus and how to pray," she added.

Just as Beth was getting ready to comment, Mandy went on, "Most of all, I want my baby to feel loved with unconditional love and to know that she is in the hands of someone she can trust. Someone who loves her so much they are willing to sacrifice anything for her."

"Wow, that's an impressive list," Beth said with a nod. She affirmed that Mandy's hopes and dreams for her baby were solid ones. She was impressed that her negative life experiences had influenced her to set positive goals for her child. Beth could see that Mandy wanted her baby to have a much better life than she had lived.

Mandy enjoyed talking with Beth. She made her feel comfortable as she gently helped her sort out her thoughts and feelings. Over the last several months, Mandy had experienced a change in almost every area of her life. She was doing a complete "about-face," as Mrs. Wilcox used to say at the girls' home she attended, when things got completely turned around. A different home, part-time work, and godly friends who were nothing like her old peers were just a few of the changes. And the most significant difference of all was that she had a personal relationship with Jesus Christ. Living her life for Jesus had changed her in every way for the better. She couldn't get enough of Him or His word. She was always hungry for more. For the first time in her life, she felt she was loved, truly loved.

The one thing that hadn't changed for Mandy was that she had no family to back her up or help her think things through. At the girls' school in her teen years, there were counselors and house parents available to her when she needed advice. She had Mrs. B now and was comfortable confiding in her, but Mrs. B was limited in her knowledge about services and programs for girls in Mandy's situation. She needed someone who would help her sort through her thoughts and make plans. She appreciated Beth's advice and genuinely felt there was no judgment from her as they talked.

Mandy commented that she admired Beth's family picture on the wall and how that modeled for her what a happy family looked like. Beth was pleased to tell her that the two little dark-skinned girls in the photo were twins they had adopted from a former client of hers. Beth beamed when she talked about what joy these two little girls had brought into their home. In fact, one of them was named Joy. Her twin sister was Faith. A real family—that was what Beth had, and not only did Mandy wish this for her baby girl, she also desired it for herself.

She left Beth's office with a few of the cobwebs cleared from her head. Beth had given her a lot of brochures and paperwork to look over. She set up an appointment to check back in a couple of weeks.

Beth was yet one more person who had come to her rescue. Rescuing seemed to be a common theme in her life these days. Mandy had always dreamt of being rescued by a knight in shining armor. In a sense, she had been. Although much different than her dreams, her knight was a fifty-year-old woman, who hadn't carried her away on horseback into the sunset. No, her knight rescued her off the steps of an abortion clinic, took her to a diner, and introduced her to a real Savior—Jesus Christ.

On her way to work, Mandy's bus drove past the abortion clinic where she'd first encountered Mrs. B a few months ago. Looking out the window as they passed she saw the faithful pro-life supporters there holding their signs and gathered in prayer. She looked to see if Mrs. Banks was there, but she didn't notice her. She thought about the morning that Mrs. B held a sign that got her attention and spoke words that changed her life. The sight of the building jogged her memory, and Mandy began to remember that day … the day that had set the rest of her life in motion.

It was a brisk fall morning the day of Mandy's appointment at the abortion clinic. She woke up anxious and tired from a recurring dream. She had never experienced such a disturbing dream as this. She typically woke up feeling exhausted because of it. Her sleep-time adventures remained in her thoughts throughout the day, and she could remember every detail vividly.

She was there looking down at the little fawn in the deep hole. The fawn's anxious mother paced back and forth, snorting and grunting and helplessly looking in at her babe. However, Mandy sensed that the doe did not feel hopeless. Had she felt hopeless, she would have left the baby there, but she didn't. The devoted momma had ventured into the woods, putting her own life at risk by approaching a human and asking the human for help in the only way she knew how. Mandy was going to help her if it took every bit of strength she had.

Not knowing what else to do, she found a stone with a jagged edge and used it to dig. She began to dig out on one side of the hole. She pulled the dirt toward her and away from the opening. She was hoping to dig down far enough that she could at last grasp some part of the fawn and hoist him up. Even though the soil was sandy, it was packed, and Mandy had great difficulty getting it to budge. She was careful not to pull back too hard, spilling more dirt on the fawn, so she chunked away little bits at a time. It was painstaking work and very time-consuming. She wasn't making much progress, but she was getting some of the sides of the hole moved above and away from the hole.

Mandy worked and worked. Her arms and back began to grow tired, and her fingers were bleeding from the sharp edges of the stone. Momma doe paced and grunted while the baby fawn lay motionless in the bottom of the hole. Mandy had moments when she felt all this work was useless. Why was she doing all this painstaking work for a dead fawn? But she would look up at the panicked eyes of the big momma doe and knew, dead or alive, this beautiful momma needed to nuzzle and sniff and touch her offspring again. Mandy wanted to be sure that she had done everything within her power to save the baby, so she pressed on.

With every few inches of earth she moved, Mandy would lay down in it and stretch her hands down into the hole as far as she could toward the fawn, but he was still far away. Sometimes, as she dug, she felt he might be sinking even more. At times, she felt the process was hopeless.

At last she lay down in the part of the hole she had dug up and reached down as far as she could without falling in herself, and her fingertips felt fur! She was very close. That little bit of softness on the ends of her throbbing fingers gave Mandy motivation to keep digging, and so she did. She dug with fresh new fervor and quickness. "Just a little bit more, Momma," she said to the doe, hoping to give her some comfort. The doe remained patient, never leaving Mandy's side.

Mandy gave one final heave to the mound of dirt she had pushed to the side and lay down one more time. She nestled herself in as far as she could on the ground and reached her hands down as far as she could. This time she could lay her whole hand on the soft fur of the fawn, and then she noticed something. Not only was the baby very soft, but he was warm! The little fawn was alive! Mandy stretched herself out as far as she could and with determination she ran her hands up and down the little fawn hoping to find something to grasp onto that she could pull him out without injury.

Mandy felt his wet little nose and realized she was near his head, so she slid her hands down the length of his neck and gave a gentle tug. She didn't know how wedged he was. To her surprise, he moved easily. She braced herself some more, hoping not to lose her grip, and pulled with all her might. This tug was enough to get the fawn on his feet or at least in a position where she could grab his front legs and pull him gently up. And up he came!

At last, she had freed the tiny fawn from his soon-to-be grave. He flinched and shivered, and Mandy managed to gather herself into a sitting position while pulling the fawn close to her. She inspected him with her hands to see if she could feel any broken bones, but he wanted nothing to do with her touch. He wriggled and writhed, trying to escape her embrace, and Mandy could feel his heart pounding next to her.

She didn't want to put him down for fear he would fall into the hole a second time. She worked at getting into an upright position while still hanging tightly to the wiggly fawn, and when she did, she came eye to eye with the big doe. The doe was already sniffing and nuzzling and licking the little one in her arms. Mandy carried the fawn to the edge of the woods, out of danger of falling into the pit again. The doe followed closely, barely letting Mandy walk.

Once she released the little one, he went straight to his mother, found her milk quickly, and began sucking hungrily. He stood steady on his spindly legs as he nursed, and Momma doe was in an awkward position trying to suckle and lick the little one all at the same time. Mandy could sense the doe's relief to have him at her side once more.

As she stood there taking in the scene, the doe stopped licking long enough to look up at Mandy. Their eyes met for a moment, and Mandy recognized the doe's thankfulness. She was thankful to have her baby back, safe, sound, and out of harm's way.

It was the conclusion of this recurring dream that stayed planted in Mandy's mind that morning, five months ago, as she readied herself to go to the clinic. She stopped at the bank on the way and withdrew her savings to add to the five hundred dollars Kade had given her to pay for the procedure.

She drove apprehensively to the clinic. Visions of the doe and the sacrifices she made to free her baby swirled in her thoughts. The sincerity in the doe's eyes remained in her mind's eye. She pulled up to the clinic for her 10:00 a.m. appointment. Once again, she was doing this alone. It wasn't the first journey she had made alone in her lifetime. For this journey, however, she wished to have some support, someone to hold her hand, to tell her it was going to be okay. There was no one. Just her … again.

There was no room in the parking lot behind the center, so she had to find a spot across the street. She didn't mind parking there, but it meant she would be forced to walk past the small pro-life group who gathered on the sidewalk outside the clinic. They carried signs with Bible verses and sayings, and Mandy dreaded walking close to them. She dreaded their judgment and what they might say to her. These "goody-goodies" with their expensive sneakers and fancy signs had no idea what it was like to walk in her shoes. She had no tolerance today for anything or anyone who might make her feel guilty about something she thought she had to do.

Her street smarts kicked in. Since Mandy always had a plan, she would use one that she learned while living on the streets. When she and her sisters were trying to avoid pimps and pushers on the streets of the city, they would lower their heads, avoid all eye contact, and walk as fast as they could. That was her plan now. She got out of her car and made a beeline for the building, with her head down. The trouble was, she had to cross the road and then walk up a couple of steps off the street onto the sidewalk before she reached the steps up to the clinic. Watching for oncoming traffic as she crossed would require her to look up, so she did.

It was in that moment of looking up that she saw the figure of Mrs. B standing there. "It was like this woman had a halo around her," Mandy often said when retelling the story. She held a sign that said simply, "You and your baby are created with PURPOSE." "You" was written in big, bold letters, and Mandy noticed it right away, but the word *purpose* stuck out to her like a sore thumb.

"'Purpose'? Maybe so," Mandy muttered while she waited on traffic. "Some purpose!" She waited for the last car to whiz by before she started moving toward the steps that led up to the sidewalk. She didn't want to make eye contact with anyone, so she put her head down and picked up her pace.

As she walked, the pro-life supporters called out to her. "Choose life for your baby." "Your baby deserves life." "Abortion is murder."

Some were calling out scriptures, and then she heard someone over the others: "God created *you*. *You* are precious to Him. Don't do this to yourself. Don't make a decision *you* will regret forever, like I did!"

These words echoed above the others and rang in Mandy's ears. The person who spoke them seemed to be concerned for her, not just for her baby. The woman seemed to be speaking from experience. The words so touched her soul that she glanced up to see who spoke them. It was the halo woman. There was just something about this woman's presence that was special. She stood out in the crowd as if she were wearing a bright, shiny halo. She held the sign about being God's handiwork, created with a purpose. *Surely this preppy, perfect-looking woman never had an abortion,* Mandy thought. She didn't seem to fit Mandy's description of how someone who'd had an abortion should look. Someone like herself; poor, unrefined, and disheveled. Mandy reckoned she was the churchy, religious type with her preppy haircut and sweater draped over her shoulders. Mandy compared her to other churchgoing people she had known in her past, who always seemed to be clean-cut and perfect.

Mandy arrived at the steps leading up to the sidewalk. With the weight of everything pressing down on her, she felt as if she had cement blocks attached to her feet. The visions of the deer and how happy she was to see her little fawn. The feeling of holding the baby fawn close to her chest and feeling his heartbeat. She tried to shrug it off as just being a dream, but it felt real to her. She couldn't forget the satisfaction and peace she had felt when she pulled the fawn from the hole and returned him to his anxious mother. Watching the reunion of mother and child stirred unfamiliar emotions in Mandy's heart.

She worked at canceling these thoughts by reminding herself that there was no way she could provide for a child. She could barely take care of herself. Having this abortion was what she had to do. But what about that sign stating that she and her baby had a purpose? What if the words from the woman telling her she would regret this decision were all true? Mandy had not put thought into any of that. What if she was carrying the next president or the person who would cure cancer? What if she was about to destroy some of God's grand plans?

Her thoughts quickly switched, and she scolded herself to think God would even care. He'd never provided for her; why would He provide for her baby. Why hadn't He ever given her a real family? If God really cared for her, if she was His handiwork, as the sign said, why was she here alone? Why would a God who cared cause this to happen? Endless questions raced through Mandy's mind as she made her way up the steps to the sidewalk. She was overwhelmed with emotion; confusion, fear, and bitterness warred in her soul. She was angry at God, if there really was a God. She was mad at Kade for betraying her, but most of all, she was put out with herself for being so foolish as to believe his lies. Feelings of disappointment and loneliness welled up inside her, and she felt as though she couldn't breathe.

It wasn't her first time to feel disappointment. Anyone she had ever cared about had let her down in life. She would not bring another person into this world whom she would most definitely let down as others had done to her. These were the thoughts that now fueled her with determination, and she mumbled, "I've got to do this!"

As soon as the words left her lips, the vision of pulling the fawn up out of the hole came to her again. It was then she realized she was sweating on this crisp autumn day.

Hunger pangs gnawed at her; she'd eaten no breakfast that morning. No money for food and terrible morning sickness had served as constant reminders of the rigors of pregnancy. It was taking a toll, not only on her body but also on her bank account. Mandy trudged on, trying to convince herself this was the only solution for her, and yet she felt an incredible tug not to go through those doors. Her mind was spinning; she was unusually sweaty, and as she got to the top step, her vision started to fade. Mandy realized she was about to pass out. She sat down quickly and put her head on her knees as she had learned to do at first-aid training in the factory.

Before she knew it, the halo woman was by her side. "Sweetie, are you okay?" she asked tenderly.

"No, no ... I think I'm going to pass out," Mandy said in a muffled voice, her head still resting on her folded arms. Waves of nausea rose in her chest.

"Honey, did you eat breakfast today?"

"No, I didn't feel like eating," Mandy said, now lifting her pale face up to the woman beside her.

"Listen, what do you say I go buy you some breakfast down the street here? You really need to eat—your blood sugar has probably bottomed out."

Mandy was hungry, and she knew she couldn't face what was inside those doors if she was already feeling faint, especially if she had to drive home. Right now, she didn't feel she could walk upright, let alone sit behind the wheel of the car. She needed this woman's help whether she wanted to admit it or not.

However, she didn't want this woman to take advantage of her weakness and talk her out of her decision. "This is just your way of trying to talk me out of going through with the abortion, isn't it?" Mandy snapped. "You're going to take advantage of my fainting to try to keep me from going in, aren't you?"

The woman was quick to respond but also honest with her reply. "First of all, I'm genuinely concerned about you and want to buy you breakfast, but I won't lie to you either. I will do everything within my power to talk you out of this because I have made this choice before, and I regret that decision every day of my life. After you eat and you're feeling better, I just want to tell you my story, and then you are free to go and choose whatever you want, I promise!"

Not physically able to move forward with her plan, she realized she was at this woman's mercy. With the woman's help, Mandy managed to stand and leaned on her as they walked to the diner two buildings down and sat in a corner booth.

"My name is Ayala Banks, by the way, but most folks just call me Mrs. B," she said as she unrolled the silverware and placed the napkin in her lap.

Mandy was still feeling light-headed but was starting to cool down and took a sip of the water in front of her. "I'm Mandy," she offered, being sure not to make eye contact.

The waitress came by, and Mrs. B assured a still-hesitant Mandy that it was okay to order. Mrs. B asked the waitress if she would bring a glass of juice to the table right away for the young woman. The mouthwatering smells wafting throughout the cafe made Mandy realize she hadn't sat down to a real meal in days.

Before long, a big stack of pancakes was sitting in front of her. Without hesitation, she slathered them with butter and rich maple syrup and dug in. They were delicious, and she could feel the color slowly returning to her cheeks after several bites.

Mrs. B noticed it too. "You're already looking better, dear. Are you feeling better?"

"Yes," Mandy replied, "I am feeling better. Thank you for helping me and buying me breakfast. And I'm sorry I snapped at you," she added.

"Oh, it's okay. I get cranky myself when I don't eat. You were in a bad way." Mrs. B didn't leave time for chitchat. She was on a mission, and she set out to make it happen. "Listen, Mandy; I'm not one to mince words," she began. "I don't know your story, I don't know where you've been, but I believe in God. I also believe that the Bible is His one true word. In His word, it says that 'we are God's handiwork, created in Christ Jesus to do good works that He has prepared in advance for us to do.' You see, Mandy, I believe with all my heart that God created all of us with a purpose in mind. He does not make mistakes. We may find our purpose early in life, we might find it late, and we may find it through some tough times. That's how I found my purpose and the direction He had for me."

Mrs. B could see that Mandy was listening intently, and so she pulled a pink bible from her backpack and flipped through the pages as she continued. "I also believe the Bible when it says, 'I know the plans I have for you, declares the Lord, plans to prosper you and not harm you, plans for a hope and a future.'" She opened her Bible wide to the book of Jeremiah and smoothed the page as she turned it for Mandy to see. She ran her finger down chapter 29 to verse 11, pointing it out to her.

She looked up and asked Mandy if she was a believer. "Well, I'm never sure what to believe about God. I learned a little about Him in some of the foster homes I lived in growing up, and I, for sure, don't know about this purpose stuff. It seems to me He's had pretty lousy plans for me, and they just keep getting worse."

She put her finger on the verse Mrs. B had pointed out and ran it over the word *prosper*. "Nothing that's happened in my life has prospered me. I've been harmed plenty, my life seems hopeless, and the future doesn't look so great either. I'm not going to drag a kid into this hopelessness; that's why I must do what I'm going to do. You don't understand what it's like to have no one and nothing. I'm doing this baby a favor by not bringing it into a life lived with me!" Mandy's voice cracked; her bitterness spilling freely like the maple syrup on her pancakes.

"Believe it or not, I can identify with what you're saying," Mrs. B replied. "I don't know what you've been through, but I do know that when I found out I was pregnant many years ago, I thought the same thing. I felt like I didn't have time for a pregnancy or a baby. I felt it would really cramp my style." Her eyes met Mandy's. "But nothing felt worse than the gaping hole that was left in my heart when I realized I had murdered my baby. I felt so guilty that I got severely depressed and almost committed suicide."

Her eyes now brimmed with tears, and Mandy could see that

recalling this memory was hard for her. "You mean you almost took your own life over your abortion?" she asked.

Mrs. B continued with her story. She went into great detail about the procedure, the signs on the sidewalk, the depression that followed days later, and her trip to the bridge. And then she told how she had been rescued, not just by Officer Banks, but by Jesus himself.

After hearing Mrs. B's story, Mandy was very confused. She had lots of questions about Jesus and salvation and why bad things happen to people. Mrs. B graciously offered to answer them all.

"So, what if I don't go through with this abortion? Then what? How in the world do I raise this baby?" Mandy's tone demanded an answer.

Mrs. B pulled a card out of her pocket and handed it to her. "I tell you what, Mandy, you come over to the Center for Hope on Thursday. It's a pregnancy resource center. We offer free testing, counseling, ultrasounds, and all kinds of services to help you make good, solid decisions for this precious life you carry. I'll be there, and I'll call them today to see if I can get the 10 a.m. appointment for you to have an ultrasound. Would that be okay? Would you like to see your baby on ultrasound, Mandy?"

"You mean it won't cost me anything?"

"No, it will cost you nothing, and we can even get you started on vitamins too while you're there," Mrs. B offered. "Those will be free as well."

Mandy was hesitant, but she finally agreed that she would meet her on Thursday at ten o'clock. Mrs. B paid the waitress, and after she put her change in her purse, she handed the pink Bible to Mandy. She told Mandy that the Bible had several pages marked for her to read. They walked back together toward the clinic so that Mandy could get her car.

Mrs. B placed her arm lightly across Mandy's shoulders as they walked. Typically, Mandy would frown at someone touching her in this way, but for some odd reason, she found this woman's touch to be very comforting to her. Walking toward her car now and not going back to the abortion clinic gave her a great sense of relief.

She was still clutching the pink Bible in one hand and the business card in the other when they arrived at her car. She glanced down at the business card to see that "Ayala Banks" was written on it along with a phone number and a verse. Mandy recognized it was the verse about "God's handiwork" Mrs. B had on her sign.

Looking at her name on the card, she was embarrassed she couldn't remember how to pronounce it. "I'm sorry, how do you pronounce your first name again?

"Ayala. Just remember, the first *a* is long, the second *a* is short, and the *y* is silent." She rolled her eyes a bit and smiled. "Now you know why most just call me Mrs. B!"

"Hmmm, it's a pretty name. I've never heard it before." Mandy tucked the card inside the Bible.

"Oh yes," Mrs. B said with a chuckle. "Well, my mother chose that name because she said when I was born I had big doe eyes. She found the name in a book—it means deer."

CHAPTER Twelve

Some time alone to stare into the Cambodian sunset was just what Skylar needed. Ever since he had read Rae's message, he just felt sick. He had spent the better part of five months in Cambodia with his study group. They had been so busy with their research and basic day-to-day survival in this unique culture that he hadn't had time to be homesick. But tonight, as he gazed blankly toward the horizon, he wished he were home more than anything else in the world.

He wanted to be with Rae. He felt sorry to have put her in this position. He was angry at himself for losing his resolve and allowing the desires of the flesh to take over in that one moment. Even more so, he was upset to have taken Rae down with him. He hated most of all that she had been going through all this alone. She hadn't even told her parents. Although Skylar was okay with that, as he wanted to be with her when she did, he knew that it must be incredibly hard on her. She typically told her parents everything; they were very close. He realized she was at a crucial point in her studies as well, and according to her message she was struggling with her classes.

Skylar tilted his head heavenward, tears slipped from the corners of his closed eyes. "Oh Father, I'm so sorry for failing You and for failing Rae!" he prayed. "Please God, help Rae to be strong, and give us a new direction in our lives together—now, as a family."

The word *family* struck him like a bolt of lightning. For the first time since discovering the news, the ramifications of all this came crashing down on him. The realization that he and Rae would be parents was incredibly hard to fathom. It was something he had always dreamt about; he'd loved Rae Carver his whole life. There was nothing he wanted more in life than to make her his wife. They both had worked long and hard to keep their relationship strong despite the distance between them. When she decided to go south to her dad's Indiana alma mater, and Skylar decided to stay in their home state of Minnesota for college, they knew it would be tough. But they had developed a plan that would help them both realize their career goals and ultimately their marriage goals. How would a baby change the course of those dreams? Skylar just shook his head thinking of it all.

Human weakness resulting in one night of passion had forever changed their plans. He and Rae weren't ready to be parents. They had so much schooling left, they didn't have an income, and worse yet, they weren't even married. Never would he have thought this could happen to him; and yet it had. How would they tell their parents? He knew their parents would be disappointed in them.

Skylar had many plans in place for when he got home; none of which included becoming a dad or having a total redo of his life. He was overwhelmed at the thought of everything, and he missed Rae desperately. He wanted to hold her close and tell her it would all be okay. That was his instinct with Rae. He always tried to protect her.

When Rae's brother, Kurt, was injured a few years ago, Skylar couldn't handle the hurt and sadness in Rae's eyes. He would have done anything to make the pain go away for her. He wanted to be by her side then, and he wanted to be there now. And even though he wanted desperately to tell her everything would be okay, he himself wasn't sure it was true. Skylar Weaver, for the first time in a long time, laid his head down on his bent knees and cried.

Skylar's faith was zapped to the core. He cried out in prayer, asking God to give him the strength to fully trust in Him and rely on His will for his life, for Rae's life and for the baby He had created through them. He mustered up the strength to thank his heavenly Father for this little life that was forming and prayed a prayer of blessing and well-being over the baby and Rae. He asked God to work out all the details for them in His perfect timing. He also prayed for forgiveness that gratitude had not been his first prayer when he heard the news. Sadly, thanking God for the gift of life had been an afterthought.

Even though Skylar would be back on American soil in a little over two weeks, he and Rae had not planned to see each other until her finals were over in mid-May. His flight would be landing in Minneapolis, and he planned to wrap things up for this semester at school, pack up his apartment, and drive a couple of hours to his home just south of the university. Then he and Rae had decided that he would come pick her up and bring her home to Minnesota for the summer. They had talked about working Bible camp again this summer, as they had in the past, but nothing was firm. The chances of that happening now were slim. He was pretty sure the directors would frown on an unwed pregnant couple mentoring the kids at Bible camp.

Skylar dropped his head into his hands in disbelief. He could hardly stand the thought that he and his girlfriend were having a baby out of wedlock. He felt ashamed. He and Rae had taught a purity class last summer to the teenagers at camp. They had both encouraged friends in college who were struggling with sexual pressures, and now … well, now he felt like a hypocrite! A big fat hypocrite! And poor Rae—she might as well have a "scarlet letter" on her chest, as he was sure that by now she was showing the signs of pregnancy. He couldn't stand the thought of telling their parents, the gossip in their town, the disappointment in their church family, and facing their peers. The fact that he had a pregnant girlfriend went against every fiber of his moral being.

But the hardest pill to swallow was that while he had been on his study abroad trip, witnessing the need in Cambodia, Skylar sensed God calling him to go into the ministry, perhaps even as a missionary. Skylar spent a lot of time with his friends praying about this "calling" laid upon his heart over the last five months. He was anxious to talk to his parents about it and seek their godly counsel. He couldn't wait to tell Rae and see what she thought about him changing his major and going to seminary when he finished school. But now he wondered if he had misread the calling on his life. Surely God wouldn't call an unwed father into ministry—or would He? Skylar felt overwhelmed, and another wave of sadness washed over him. He fell over, face down on the grass, crying out to Jesus in prayer until he fell asleep under the moonlit Cambodian sky.

CHAPTER
Thirteen

The day Ayala had been waiting for had finally arrived. The sun was out, the weather forecast looked like the threat of frost was over, and she had recruited two young women to help her. Her potting shed was full of hearty plants and beautiful flowers. She couldn't wait to dig in the fertile soil and plant them. There was something very satisfying to Ayala about planting a garden, nurturing it, and watching it grow. Plucking hearty, ripe vegetables from the vine was a thrill for her. It gave her great pleasure to partake in the fruits of her labor. It reminded her of a favorite Bible verse, Galatians 6:8, about reaping what you sow: "Whoever sows to please their flesh, from the flesh will reap destruction; whoever sows to please the Spirit, from the Spirit will reap eternal life." If you sow good things, more good things will come.

Ayala felt like she had been doing a lot of "sowing" lately. Although she understood she wouldn't always see the harvest of what she had sown, she felt honored to have a small part in Mandy's and Rae's growth. She loved these girls dearly. She especially had a soft spot for Mandy, having drawn especially close to her in the last couple of months. Ayala loved the late-night chats they had when Rae was busy studying.

Mandy had endured more than her fair share of heartache in her young life. Here she was, about to be a mother, when she hadn't even had a mother for most of her life. She knew that Mandy had a sincere desire to be mentored, nurtured, and mothered by someone. Having the guidance and direction of parents was something most people took for granted.

Many times in her youth, Ayala had been ashamed of her parents. She had disrespected them and thought their demands were insensitive or old fashioned. She regretted all that now. Undoubtedly, her soul would have been tormented forever had she not had the chance to ask their forgiveness later in life. Before they died, she and Tim had made many good memories with them, even though her dad spent his last years in a nursing home. She was privileged to help care for both in their later years. Having met Mandy and heard her story, she appreciated the gift of her parents' guidance in her life even more.

But mostly Ayala loved her time with Mandy because it made her feel like she was a mother. Ayala had always longed for a daughter. Her abortion took that hope away from her. After three miscarriages, doctors discovered that Ayala had some abortion-related scar tissue in her uterus that kept her from carrying a baby to term. Eventually, she and Tim decided that they wouldn't even try anymore because it was too heartbreaking each time. They had considered adoption and toyed with the idea of being foster parents but for various reasons never pursued either. Ayala regretted that now and sorely missed having a child.

Many times, while Tim was battling cancer, she wished she'd had an adult child to walk through this valley with her. She often thought it would have been special to have someone to be his legacy, to help her make decisions, and provide companionship to her now that he was gone. She felt alone, and there were many things in life she regretted or wished she could do over.

Having Mandy and Rae around had given her a sense of the nurturing she had longed to give over the years. She loved their friendship, their time cooking meals together, and their crazy card games, and she especially loved when they prayed together. Their prayer time had become something they all looked forward to. Mandy was just beginning to feel comfortable about praying out loud, and every time Mandy poured her heart out to God, Ayala couldn't help but cry. Mandy … talking to her Savior! It was such a glorious thing, and Ayala's heart felt like it might burst with joy every time she heard her pray.

Mandy was learning more each day about who she was in Christ. The old Mandy blamed God for all the things that had gone wrong in her life. But through Bible study and searching the scriptures together, the new Mandy was starting to understand that it was God who rescued her every time she faced difficulty in life. From the foster homes she stayed in, to the meals that neighbors had offered when her mother wasn't around, to the home she now shared with Ayala and Rae, Mandy was seeing where God had been there for her through all of it. She was reveling in the joy of her salvation and understanding that Christ was sufficient for all her needs. She was an inspiration to Ayala, and Ayala loved her.

Ayala had much love and affection for Rae also. Who wouldn't? Rae's name suited her well, as she was such a ray of sunshine to all who knew her. Even though Ayala had encouraged her to speak to her parents about her baby, she understood her desire to wait on Skylar. Ayala didn't worry about Rae the way she worried about Mandy. She knew that Rae had the support and love that would see her and her baby through. Rae would be okay, but she was just as anxious as Rae was for Skylar to get home and get things figured out so she could move forward and enjoy her pregnancy without the stress and worry of the unknown.

She looked forward to seeing their babies and what lay ahead of them in their future. But for now, she was going to put them to work.

She laid out three pairs of gloves and was making quite a commotion trying to gather the rakes and hoes from their winter bed in the shed. Mandy and Rae came to investigate what all the ruckus was about. They seemed to be excited when Mrs. B said they were going to plant a garden.

"Oh, I used to love to play in the dirt and make mud pies while my mother planted," Rae mused.

"Would you like me to go get some pie pans and water for you, Rae, so you can make us some pies for dinner?" Ayala teased.

"None for me, thanks!" added Mandy with a grimace.

Ayala handed Rae a hoe and said slyly, "Let's see if you can use a hoe as well as you can make mud pies!"

Rae took the hoe by the metal end, letting the handle rest on the ground, and asked, with a twisted grin, "Like this, Mrs. B?"

Ayala gave her a sideways glance and rolled her eyes toward Mandy. "Looks like we've got our work cut out for us with this one," she said, laughing.

Mandy giggled. "Well, quite honestly, Mrs. B, I might actually do that and not be joking; I don't know the first thing about gardening. City girls are all about concrete, ya know? No dirt in my background except what was on the floor of our apartment!" she said with a turned-up nose.

"No worries, girls! I'll make you into little farmers yet!" Ayala beamed with confidence.

"Umm, 'little' farmers?" Rae mused while pointing to Mandy's big belly.

At that, Mandy teasingly slapped Rae on the backside with her gloves and reminded her that she wasn't "Skinny Minnie" herself these days.

Ayala laughed out loud at these silly girls. She loved this playful banter and the joy they brought her. "Okay, you two, let's get crackin'," she said as she handed Mandy a tray of vegetable starts. She gave them direction as to where she wanted each start planted, and the three of them went to work in the warm early May sun. Vegetables and flowers weren't the only things "sown" that day.

CHAPTER Fourteen

Beth Tudor entered the local diner to find her noon appointment, Mandy Lewis, sitting in a booth on the other side. She had many items to share with Mandy today. Mandy had a lot on her plate. There were significant decisions to make, and Beth wanted to ensure she gave godly counsel and gentle guidance.

Beth wanted to help Mandy in every aspect of her planning for her future. In talking with Mandy, she realized that parenting a child would be difficult for her, as she hadn't received proper parenting herself. As for financially providing for this child—well, Mandy was plainly struggling where finances were concerned. Government assistance would help, but it wouldn't be enough. No matter how Beth pushed the pencil, Mandy would have a have a hard time making ends meet.

Beth wondered how she would be doing if Ayala Banks hadn't stepped in. Ayala's generosity to give Mandy free room and board was indeed a blessing. Beth was especially glad Ayala had convinced her to enroll in classes at the Center for Hope. The courses offered there were wonderful resources for women who found themselves in these situations. They had helped her prepare and be ready for her little girl's birth and beyond. Mandy needed that. Mandy's future was uncertain, but Beth was confident of one thing regarding Mandy Lewis; she loved her baby more than she loved life itself. Beth noticed that Mandy often stroked her tummy affectionately. She remembered doing that herself when she was pregnant.

Mandy had expressed to Beth many times over that she wanted to give this baby the best life she could, no matter what it took. She had pledged her love for this little one many times over and said she was blessed to have the privilege to bring her into the world. Mandy was such an inspiration to Beth. Many of the girls Beth had helped in the past had little or no connection with their babies and frequently seemed to care more about themselves. But Beth understood fully that Mandy Lewis had her baby's best interest at heart.

Mandy noticed Beth from across the room and gave a smile and a wave. Beth flashed her big grin at Mandy. She slid into the booth across from her and looked at her, bright-eyed.

"Hey Mandy, are you hungry? I've heard their spinach salad is the best!" Beth opened the menu and began to scan the choices.

Mandy licked her lips. "Umm, I'm thinking about soup and a sandwich and, of course, ice cream!"

Beth giggled. "Well, as long as you don't have a side of pickles with that!"

"Hmm, sounds tempting," Mandy teased.

After they placed their orders with the waitress, Beth pulled out her iPad and poked in her passcode. "Well, Mandy, have you had a chance to look over all the information I sent home with you?"

Mandy nodded. "I've looked at everything, over and over! There is just too much to think about. I want to make good decisions for her," she said laying her hand on her midsection with a loving glance at her rounded belly.

"More than anything, Beth, I do not want my daughter raised the way I was," she said, her voice trailing off. Now full of emotion, she went on, "I don't want my daughter ever to have to wonder if her mom is coming home or where her next meal is coming from. She must never be separated from her loved ones, feeling like no one cares for her. I want so much more for her than I can give her," she continued. "I want to make sure I am putting things in place so that my daughter always knows, without a shadow of a doubt, that she is loved unconditionally."

With misty eyes, Beth reached across the table and gave Mandy's hand a gentle squeeze. "Mandy, I love your passion. I love your devotion to this child. I admire and respect you so much for the sacrifices you are willing to make to ensure the best for your baby." With both hands now on Mandy's, "I want you to know, for a girl who didn't have much of an example to follow for motherhood, you exemplify what motherhood is truly about."

The words Beth spoke and her sincere tone warmed Mandy's heart, and she broke into deep sobs. Her shoulders shook as she continued to clutch Beth's hand. She eventually released her grasp and reached for her napkin, dabbed at her eyes, and blew her nose. She let out a big sigh and looked up at Beth, who gazed at her with concern in her eyes.

"Oh, Beth," Mandy attempted to speak, her voice still shaking, "I can't tell you what that means to me. A lot of the times I feel like I'm just a selfish mother like my mom was. I mean, I can't even take care of her—just like my mom couldn't take care of me!"

"No, Mandy, don't let yourself go there, please," Beth looked at her earnestly. "Unselfish mothers do whatever it takes to make sure their babies have the best life they can, and Mandy, that is you!"

Mandy perked up at her words. "Just like the doe in my dreams!"

"What? Did you say the doe in your dreams?"

"Yes, I guess I haven't told you about that. If it hadn't been for that unselfish doe, Mrs. B might not have been able to keep me from returning to the abortion clinic." She sipped some water and continued, "Now don't think I'm crazy, but the Lord guides me through my dreams. He started guiding me before I even knew who He was. I had a recurring dream in the days before my trip to the abortion clinic." She brushed a stray tendril of hair from her brow. "And I continue to have it."

Beth sat up straight in her seat, "No, you didn't mention it, but I'm on the edge of my seat waiting to hear about it."

Their lunch arrived, and as they ate, Mandy shared details of her dream about the doe and the fawn in the woods.

She set her fork beside her plate. "You see, Beth ... I was so impressed by the love, compassion, and sacrifice of the doe. The satisfaction and peace I felt in the dream after rescuing the fawn— well, I feel that was the Lord speaking to me. In talking with Mrs. B and some others that I've shared the dream with, I realize now that God used the dream to rescue my baby and me."

Feeling satisfied, she pushed her plate away and continued with her story. "Then I show up at the clinic, sick and starving and just plain messed up! I was in such a bad way that day, with everything going on, that I literally got sick and almost passed out. And there was Mrs. B—to the rescue! She rushed to take care of me there on the steps of the clinic. She cared enough about me to take care of my physical needs by feeding me, but she also cared about my future needs as well. Never has anyone cared for me like that, and she was a total stranger! In those moments, she cared for me in ways that I had never experienced."

Tears filled Mandy's eyes again. "So you say I haven't had anyone set much of an example for me, but in a sense, I have had an example of true motherhood. I've had it through Mrs. B ... and the crazy thing is that she's never even been a mom herself.

"You see, Beth," Mandy continued, "I can't help but feel that God was preparing me for the months ahead in my life through the dream and through sending Mrs. B to me. I'm learning that I have a Father, and He provides for me even when I don't even realize it."

"Do you mind telling me about your mother, Mandy? Do you know what became of her?" Beth ventured to ask.

"Well, I don't really like to talk about what happened, but maybe you should know." The pain of the memory was visible in her eyes.

"It's okay, Mandy. I don't have to know unless you feel you want to share it."

"No, it's fine. It's a horrible time in my life, and I try not to think about it much. But maybe it would be good if you knew this part of my life. I've only told a few other people."

She made herself comfortable in her seat and settled in to tell Beth about the darkest day in her past.

"You see, my sisters and I were bounced around from one foster home to another. Just when we would get settled, Mom would go to the social worker and make promises she couldn't keep. We'd have visits with her, and it would seem she was really trying, and we would eventually move back in with her." Her eyes now took on a faraway look. "I don't know. I mean ... I feel like my mother loved us, but sometimes we felt she loved heroin more.

"I'll never forget the last time I saw her. The worst night of my life. She needed a fix in the worst way. She got real nervous and short tempered with us, like she did whenever she needed a fix. She sat my sisters and me down and told us that she had some friends coming over, and then she explained to us in detail what we were to do for these friends—men friends." She stressed the last two words with air quotes.

"The things she was asking us to do were just awful. Well, she wasn't even asking us. She was telling us this was what would happen—this was what we were going to do. But worst of all, she tried to justify it all by telling us we could share the money they paid and buy some new clothes with it." Disgust showed on her face. "There ain't enough new clothes in the world to cover up a body that's been robbed of its dignity like that; especially young bodies like ours!"

"Did your mother often ask you to do these kinds of things?" Beth asked, visibly shocked.

"No, this was the first time. She was that desperate for a fix." Mandy lightly pounded her fists on the table. "The girls and I knew she was in the habit of selling herself for dope money, but we never in a million years thought she'd stoop low enough to sell us too. Can you imagine wanting to shoot a drug in your veins so bad that you'd do that to your babies, Beth?"

"No, I can't imagine. How terrible for you and your sisters. So what happened?" She was almost afraid to ask.

"Well, it was at that moment that I finally gave up on my mother. I never fully trusted her anyway. I mean, I always really wanted to. I wanted her to love us bad. I wanted her to act like a real mom. I held on to any glimmer of hope that she would one day turn the corner, and we would be a real family. But finally, on this day, I gave up on her."

Mandy had tried for years to block this memory from her mind. Sometimes at night when she lay in bed or when her mind was idle, the memory would creep back. When this happened, she pushed it as far from her mind as she could. But over the last months, after Mrs. B opened her home and heart to her, Mandy confided in her to the extent of sharing this part of her story. She found it to be cathartic to share it with someone who cared about her. In the past, if someone had asked her about this, she would have run away. But today she wasn't afraid to share it with Beth. She almost felt the need to share it—to speak it again. Maybe it was just part of her healing process, the renewal she had been experiencing recently. She took a deep breath, looked Beth in the eye, and told her about the day she would never forget, no matter how hard she tried.

You see, my mother had me by a guy she didn't even know. So for the first three years of my life, I was passed back and forth from one person or another. I never really knew my grandparents, even though I knew I had them, and I'm pretty sure I have aunts and uncles too. My mom didn't have a relationship with them, so neither did we.

Mom had a small box she kept in her sock drawer wherever we moved. When she would leave us home alone, my sisters and I would take it out and look at the pictures in it. We never told her we did this and wouldn't dare have her catch us. They were older pictures with what seemed to be her family. One of the girls in the photo looked a lot like my sister Erin, who resembles my mom the most of us three. My sisters and I assumed it was her family.

We used to look at the pictures and make up stories about the people in them. We gave them names and pretended they lived in fancy houses with carpet and ate three meals a day! It's how you entertain yourself when you're left alone a lot. My mom worked odd jobs off and on but could never keep anything steady because of her addictions, so we moved all over the place.

So, when I was around three years old, Mom brought this guy home with her one day. His name was Hank, and he was nice enough. He always called me Cookie and was kind to me for the most part, from what I can remember. Hank came around now and then and eventually he and my mom had my sisters. My sisters are just fifteen months apart in age. Hank and Mom were never married, but my sisters were brought up calling him Dad. I was always told just to call him Hank.

Sometimes, Hank would take Erin and Krista with him and go away for several days. I guess he was a good enough dad when he was around, but we didn't see him much. Hank liked to drink, and he went through as many jobs as my mom did. He did help my mom get a reasonably nice apartment once. We stayed there with Hank coming and going when he needed a "fix" of what Mom could give him. He was usually there just long enough to bounce Erin and Krista on his knee and pat me on the head and be gone again.

If he stayed very long, he and Mom would fight like crazy. They were always yelling and screaming at each other, and Hank would end up leaving, slamming doors and cursing all the way out, calling my mom every name in the book. Finally, the drinking caught up with Hank, and he landed in jail. I never knew why exactly, but I knew it had to do with driving while intoxicated. So Hank was in the slammer for a while, my mom couldn't make rent, and we began to live like nomads again—wandering from one place to the next. It was a vicious cycle, and my sisters and I were caught up in it big time.

So my little sisters depended on me. There were many times we were left alone. Sometimes she would leave after we went to sleep, and we wouldn't see her again until late the next day. A couple of times we put ourselves to bed the second night too, usually without having eaten much. Those were the times we often ended up in foster homes. But we looked after each other, especially after Hank went to jail. My mom changed after that, and life was … well, it was just plain hard.

I was getting ready for my sophomore year of high school, Erin was twelve, and Krista was eleven when my mom got desperate enough to sell our bodies for a fix. Hank had just gotten out of jail a few weeks before this, and somehow he had found my mom and came to visit the girls. The girls were happy to see him. And I was too for some odd reason. Hank was never really anything to me, but he made my sisters happy, and my mom seemed to be happier when he was around, so I was glad to see him.

But seeing him this time didn't make my mom happy. By this time she was so deep in her addiction that all she wanted from Hank was a child support check. So she immediately started in on him about getting a job and starting to support his kids. She threatened never to let him see the girls again if he didn't start paying up.

Hank made promises to Mom that we all knew he wouldn't be able to keep, but she kicked him out and told him not to come back until he had cash in hand. He told Erin and Krista that he loved them and would try his hardest to get a job. He claimed that being locked up had changed him, and he wanted to turn over a new leaf. After he said his goodbyes, he mentioned to Mom that he was staying at the homeless shelter on the west side of town if they needed him; and he went. Erin and Krista were so sad and begged Mom to let them see him, but she just ignored them.

A couple of weeks went by, and Mom got more agitated and shaky, and she stayed away for long periods. Every time she left, she'd be all dressed up and be wearing the perfume from the cabinet that we were forbidden to wear. She usually came home after a couple of days in a better mood, until she needed her fix again, and then the agitation, nervousness, and craziness would start all over.

Apparently, after one of her outings, her sugar daddy wasn't satisfied with her anymore and wanted us! So, it was on that day that my mother, my own flesh and blood, the woman who carried me for nine months and gave birth to me, decided that a shot of heroin in her veins was way more important to her than us, and she agreed to the arrangement.

After she sat us down and told us in graphic detail what we were to do and how we were to do it and all the rewards we would get for doing these horrible things, we were completely mortified. Living on the streets, I had heard of these things and knew that people did this kind of stuff, but my sisters weren't as wise to it as I was. Of course, they were terrified at the mere thought of such actions. In fact, Krista began to cry and scream at Mom that she was not going to do it, and Mom couldn't make her.

And then my mom went too far. Now my mom was a lot of things, and she was never a good mother, but she had never struck us. Yelled at us? Yes. Called us horrible names? Yes. But she had never hit us. When Krista stood up to our mother like that, she hauled off and slapped Krista right across the face. It was a loud, forceful slap, and Krista grabbed her face and fell into a heap on the floor. Then my mother turned into a monster and began to kick Krista and punch her and totally unleashed on her. Erin and I jumped to her defense, and we started yelling for Mom to stop. We were screaming at Krista to run, but she just stayed there, curled up in a ball, letting Mom kick her and pound on her back with her fists.

Mandy's face became red with rage; her bottom lip trembled as she spoke. Her voice grew quiet, and through gritted teeth, she continued. Beth could tell it was difficult for Mandy to recount the story.

"I was so angry at my so-called mother and the monster she had become. I couldn't believe she would do this to poor, sweet, innocent Krista. I grew so enraged that I lost control and grabbed a baseball bat that we kept behind the door. It was our security system, I guess you'd say. And I took that baseball bat without any second thoughts, and I began to beat my mother with it. And I think I would have kept hitting her if Erin had not stopped me after Mom dropped to the ground. She just lay there. I felt like my heart was going to pound out of my chest. I ditched the bat, scooped Krista up off the ground, and grabbed Erin by the hand, and we got out of there as fast as we could.

"We had no clue where Hank's homeless shelter was, but that was where we hoped to end up. We had no idea what to do. We had to help Krista walk. She was so beaten up, walking slowly and not wanting to continue for the fourteen or so blocks to the shelter. Pretty soon a policeman spotted us. I'm sure we were a sight to see, dragging our crying, hobbling sister down the street. When he stopped to ask us if we were okay, we told him what happened. I told him everything, and I confessed to him that I thought I'd killed our mother." Mandy paused, the enormity of the memory tugging at her heartstrings and filling her eyes with tears.

Beth stared at Mandy with shock and horror on her face, her hands folded high on her chest as if she was trying to keep her heart from jumping out of it. She couldn't believe how this sweet girl before her had fended off her own mother for her sister's sake. She couldn't imagine all that Mandy had endured in her lifetime. "Oh, no, Mandy, so your mother … your mother has passed?" Beth asked with caution.

"No—don't worry, I didn't kill her. Everything is kind of a blur from there. Krista was checked out at the hospital, and we were all taken to a foster home. The officer went back to the apartment expecting to find Mom dead. He found her beaten up and her male friends there with her. They had arrived for their 'fun fling' and found Mom on the floor. They all ended up getting arrested.

"The weeks that followed were the worst weeks of my life. The authorities contacted Hank, and he came and claimed Erin and Krista and took them with him. He had found a job and an apartment in the city. He apologized to me that he couldn't take me too, but he just didn't think he could afford all three of us. It was going to be a stretch for him to support Erin and Krista.

"Saying goodbye to my sisters was incredibly hard on all three of us. Hank promised we'd see each other again, but just like Hank's other promises, that never came true. The last I knew, he and the girls moved to Missouri. I lost contact with them. And sadly, I don't even know Hank's last name to try and find them. My sisters always went by Lewis, like me. I've tried looking them up on social media, but nothing. I was left as a ward of the state and taken to a girls' home where I finished school, got a job in high school, and learned to support myself."

Beth marveled at the courage and tenacity of this young woman in front of her. "Oh, Mandy, I can't imagine what grief and uncertainty you've faced in your young lifetime. Do you know whatever happened to your mom?"

"I was told by my caseworker that my mother had signed over her parental rights of me to the state and would be in prison for a few years. I missed my sisters terribly, and I cried for them every day for weeks on end, but, for the most part, my time at the girls' home was okay. For the first time in my life, I was safe and comfortable, fed and cared for. I didn't have to look out for my sisters or wonder where their next meal would come from or how they'd get medical care when they were sick or protect them from rats and roaches and freezing nights. The couple who ran the home were very nice people, and I owe them a lot for all they did for me while I was there. But they've cared for a lot of girls like me in their time. I'm sure they'd welcome me with open arms if I went back, but after I left there, I didn't want to burden them anymore, so I severed my ties with them, by choice."

"Mandy, I have goose bumps from your story. You have such amazing examples in your life of the Romans 5 verse." Beth selected the Bible application on her iPad and scrolled down to find the verse so she could read it to her.

"'Not only so, but we also glory in our sufferings, because we know that suffering produces perseverance; perseverance, character;

and character, hope. And hope does not put us to shame, because God's love has been poured out into our hearts through the Holy Spirit, who has been given to us.'

"That's Romans chapter 5, verses 3 through 5. You see, Mandy, God has been using this suffering in your life. He's been building your character through your perseverance, giving you hope. Don't waste this suffering in your life. Use it—use it to honor and glorify God."

"I'm not sure what that all means, but I do like the sound of it. I never dreamed that anything good could come from these horrible things in my past, but if I can somehow use it to help someone else—I want to."

Beth grabbed Mandy's hands and looked her in the eye. "You're right. Surely God has been preparing you through all this for your future. Keep seeking Him and asking for His guidance in your plans. He has set those plans for you. You were born with His blueprint. He has big things planned for you. I am sure He is well pleased with the great details and plans you're making."

Beth assured her, "He is there with you every step of the way, and I promise you, Mandy, so am I!" She gave her hands a gentle squeeze. "You inspire me, Miss Lewis. Thank you for sharing your story; I know it's not easy."

Mandy squeezed back and responded with a half-smile. She felt comfortable talking to Beth, as if she could tell her anything.

Beth pulled out more paperwork for her to look over, and she promised to do so. Beth also encouraged her to pray about it and have some definite answers by their next meeting. There was much for her to think about, and Beth was helping her with each aspect. Even though these decisions kept her awake at night, Mandy was determined to provide for her little girl as best she could. It was hard for her to trust, but she felt comfortable relying on Beth's expertise. Most of all, she sensed that Beth's heart was genuine, and her intentions were strictly to help her and not harm her.

Mandy left their meeting feeling assurance and peace, filled with love for the little girl who kicked and moved inside her tummy.

She shot up a quick prayer of thanksgiving to God for sending yet one more angel to help her right now during one of the hardest times of her life.

"Oh, and God," she added, "show me how to use my suffering for You."

CHAPTER Fifteen

Rae Carver had never experienced such stress in her life. The only thing that was getting her through this day was that Skylar would be home in two days. At long last, she would hear his voice. She couldn't wait!

Her last exam was difficult. Even though she had studied, she struggled when taking it, which was evident in the grade posted online today. She brought up her email and drafted a note to her professor. If he didn't give her a little grace on the grade, she would fail his class, and her scholarship would be void.

Over the last month, Rae had stayed up late every night studying and doing whatever she could to make the grade in her other classes. It had paid off, as her grades were holding steady now, and it appeared that she would ace those just in time. This physics class, however, was causing her high anxiety. She knew she had not given it adequate study time. She also regretted that she had missed some prenatal classes at the Center for Hope because of all the cramming.

She didn't tell Mrs. B or Mandy, but she had also missed her last doctor's visit as well. She had been up all night and fell asleep just an hour before the appointment and failed to wake up in time. Although she had rescheduled, she couldn't get in until next week. That was okay; her week was jam-packed with just trying to finish this semester on top. Even though decision making had not been her strong suit lately, she had concluded that this week would be devoted to her classes. Looking ahead, she realized the week might have enough stress of its own. With Skylar coming home, it would be a time to focus on their imminent future. Just figuring out the next step would be a relief to Rae. She felt like she was still paddling in her hypothetical boat, hoping to land safely on shore sometime soon.

She'd been having a lot of headaches lately, which she blamed on stress and lack of sleep, but because she didn't want to risk taking anything for fear it would harm the baby, she had a hard time getting rid of them. Sometimes, they were so intense her vision was blurred, and she had to take a moment just to stretch or close her eyes. Often, when she did that, she ended up catnapping, which took time away from her studies.

She finished her email to the professor, hoping she didn't sound too much like a desperate, unwed pregnant girl, who was trying to keep her parents happy and keep her head above water. Hopefully, he would have some mercy on her and offer her a redo of the exam or some extra credit. "Well, I actually am a desperate, pregnant, unwed mother," she muttered under her breath, sarcastically. "Why should I come off as anything but that? I hope he likes those kinds of people."

One thing Rae had missed the most in the last few weeks, due to her studying, was time with her roomies. She had put off her ice cream dates with Mandy. All the gardening had fallen on the shoulders of Mrs. B and Mandy, but they were gracious through it all.

She looked at the clock. Her heart skipped a beat when she realized that Skylar was most likely on the first leg of his return trip by now. By this time tomorrow, she hoped to hear from him somehow. She so wished she could just go to bed and sleep until then; she was crazy exhausted, and her head throbbed.

She closed her laptop and tucked it in her backpack. She tidied up her workspace on the library table and set a book aside to return to the cart. Her phone buzzed where it was nestled in a side pocket of her bag. The text message displayed on the front was from her dad. "What time does Sky get in tomorrow?" it read. Rae texted back the time with a smiley face, offering her dad no more info.

It seemed he was good at making small talk first, and then he started in with his dad digging. She didn't want to get into another exchange with him as she had on the phone a couple of nights ago when he called her. She had explained to him that she was doing an all-nighter, but he continued to question her. He had asked her about her plans for the summer and whether she wanted to work at the pharmacy over the long break. When she told him she and Skylar might be working at camp this summer, he began to dig into whether she had contacted the camp director.

"No dad, I haven't yet," she snipped at him, "because I'm waiting to see what Skylar is thinking, he may have other plans now."

Then he began his responsibility speech on how she shouldn't leave the camp director wondering because he was probably trying to plan for the summer by now and she needed to be contacting him. It was just his way of making sure she was still crossing all her t's and dotting all her i's, but it annoyed her. Especially now, because she was uncertain about how anything was going to go in her summer, and she didn't want to lie to him one more time. She was abrupt with him and ended the conversation with her typical "I love you more." She emphasized how she was cramming for exams right now and hoping her parents wouldn't bother her again until she had a chance to talk to Skylar.

Ting. Her phone chimed again. "How did your physics exam go?" he texted back. Again, Rae lied to him: "IDK, still waiting for results." She hated doing it, but she couldn't tell him the results. She was hoping the prof would get back with her and let her make it up. She was hoping she could just tell her dad she'd passed with flying colors, as usual, and the details of how she had gotten there could remain unspoken.

She had laid out so many lies over recent months with her parents that she couldn't keep up anymore. When she moved in with Mrs. B and Mandy, she stretched that as well, saying she had found cheaper rent with other friends. *Well, part of that is true*, she reasoned with herself, trying to justify it all.

There was a Bible verse Rae had learned years ago at church camp that echoed in her thoughts a lot lately: Numbers 32:23: "But if you fail to do this, you will be sinning against the LORD; and you may be sure that your sin will find you out." She was fearful that this tangled web of lies she had been weaving was sure to find her. But with Skylar's return trip beginning, she breathed a little easier, knowing that very soon the truth could be revealed. Each time she prayed, she asked God for His forgiveness and His mercy and promised that she would make right all these lies she had been telling.

Rae stood up to stretch her aching back. All the sitting and cramming had caused a strange new ache in her back, and she had to get up and walk several times or change her position to get some relief. Now six months along, she could see that her tummy had noticeably popped out the last couple of weeks. She placed one hand on her aching back and one on her rounded belly as she stretched and walked toward the periodicals to see if she could find an article for her research.

Today's newspaper sat on the top counter. As always, the sidebar contained the obituaries. It wasn't Rae's habit to look at them, but one name on the list stuck out to her: Patrice Lewis. "Hmmm, how do I know Patrice Lewis?" Rae wondered out loud. The name was strangely familiar to her, but she couldn't quite place a finger on it. She opened the paper and began to scan articles, looking for anything she could use for her research. And true to form, she got sidetracked by interesting articles she wanted to read. Her eyes caught an advertisement for a sale at her favorite shoe store and a recipe for barbecued ribs. "Wow, those would taste great about now," she mumbled as she scanned the paper.

Homeless woman found dead on Market Street now identified.

This headline on the third page caught Rae's attention. And there it was again: *Patrice Lewis*. The name seemed to jump off the page at Rae. "Well, if she was a homeless woman I'm pretty sure I didn't know her," she whispered to herself. But still something about the name struck her as familiar.

She browsed the article to find out that a woman who appeared to be a "bag lady" was found dead on the corner of Market and Fourth Street. People claimed to have seen her around, and she was known as a homeless person who seemed to have no place or purpose in life. "How sad," Rae whispered. Authorities had found some ID she'd left at a homeless shelter and had determined she was Patrice Lewis. The article noted that authorities were looking for any family or friends, anyone who might have known her.

Rae just couldn't imagine the journey this woman must have traveled. She was fortunate to have such a wonderful and loving family. She couldn't wait to get beyond all these secrets and lies and come into the light with her family because she loved them so much. All this secrecy was getting the best of her. She couldn't imagine dying as a lonely woman on a sidewalk with no support system around her.

Her thoughts meandered to her new friend Mandy. Mandy's life was similar. She didn't think Mandy would die a lonely homeless woman, but she felt so sorry for her friend that she had no support network around her as she did. She did have Mrs. B now, and Rae was thankful for the relationship the two of them had. Mandy was getting much-needed nurture from Mrs. B and the Center for Hope and now the counselor, Beth, she had been seeing. It occurred to Rae that while Mandy was on her journey of becoming a mother, along the way she had gained mothers as never before. It was a lovely thought, and yet her heart still ached for Mandy. It was hard to imagine Mandy's experience, not having the love of her mother growing up.

At that thought, Rae gasped. It was as if a light bulb had switched on in her brain, and she suddenly realized how she knew the name Patrice Lewis. "That's it!" she shrieked, a little too loudly in the library. She rushed to grab up her personal belongings. She ran out of the library and across the hallway to the bookstore to purchase today's paper.

She needed to show Mandy this newspaper. She needed to show Mandy that her mother, Patrice Lewis, had died.

CHAPTER Sixteen

Even though his day had gotten off to a rocky start, Skylar was glad this day had finally arrived. This was the part of the journey that he hated the most, riding in the tiny, rickety plane that retrieved him and his study partners from the scattered villages of the Khmer Loeu people in the highlands of Cambodia. They flew above the provinces of Ratanakiri, Stung Teng, and the Mondulkiri, where he had spent the last several months soaking in every bit of their culture, learning their differences and similarities, eating the food they worked hard for, and roughing it in the team's small rough-hewn dwelling at their campsite.

Skylar had spent these last several months in a completely different world. He had kept a diary of each day and couldn't wait to share it all with Rae. Living among these people with their tribal ways was a sharp contrast to how he was used to living in his technology-filled world. It was hard to adjust to at first, but he soon learned to appreciate the simplicity of gathering and making his dinner, of bathing himself and doing his laundry at the same time in a natural stream. Spending downtime with the villagers or sitting around a campfire with his buddies had become commonplace. He began to be content and comfortable with it. So comfortable, in fact, that he was sure he had heard God calling him to mission work. Something just felt right about being there with those people and in their villages so far from home.

Since he had read Rae's message and learned of her pregnancy, though, the news had taken over his thoughts lately. He had not slept much since then and hadn't told anyone. He had prayed about it a lot and, through much reflection, concluded that there was only one thing to do when he got home: propose. Propose to the girl of his dreams, his lifelong friend, the one he wanted to spend the rest of his life with, the beautiful woman who would soon be the mother of his child.

He needed to make this right, somehow. If they could just have a small ceremony with their pastor and family, then they would be married when their baby was born. He just couldn't fathom the thought of bringing his son or daughter into the world without being married to his or her mother. So in one of his sleepless nights, he decided that as soon as he saw Rae, he would get down on one knee, ask her to be his wife, and then get married as quickly as possible. After the baby was born, he figured, they could have a second, "real" wedding—the one he knew Rae had dreamt of since she was the "Bible study bride," way back when her best friend, Sadie, used to marry them on top of the toy box.

All of this put Skylar's mind at ease, and he began to set his plan in motion. He patted his shirt pocket to make sure the bamboo bag he had slipped in it earlier was still snug inside. The bag contained a ring he had purchased at a Cambodian market when they first arrived in the area. He knew he wouldn't have a chance to pick up a souvenir for Rae once they went into the hill country. He had picked up a beautiful handcrafted jade ring for her. It was a little more expensive than he planned, but the stone reminded him of her eyes, and he just knew she would love it. He had no idea then that he would use it as an engagement ring until he could officially get a job and purchase a real diamond for her. He decided to keep it with him as he traveled; if his luggage got lost, he'd still have the ring.

Sweat beads began to pop up on his brow—mostly from the stuffy confines of the plane cabin they had been sitting in for quite a long time, but also from the thought of proposing, marriage, getting a job, not being a missionary, and especially becoming a dad.

The plane was tiny, and rust covered its wing tips. The morning had been quite stormy, and the pilot had told them, in his broken dialect, he was waiting to be cleared for takeoff from his base. Even though the monsoon season had begun, it was still unseasonably warm, making things feel very humid. Skylar prayed a quick prayer that he and his friends wouldn't get sick on the flight. They had all felt quite queasy when they arrived several months earlier, after the flight from Thailand on the small plane.

Once they reached Thailand, they would get a bigger plane for the next leg of the trip. Skylar was in for a long day, and he was glad to be sleep-deprived, hoping that he would nap most of the time.

At last, the pilot had the okay to fly. Skylar's buddy, Mark, gave him a thumbs-up and said with a smirk, "Let's get this party started!" Five seatbelts clicked simultaneously, and the guys nestled in for the ride. Devin stared straight ahead, already gripping the seat. He had suffered the most from the last trip, having been sick for a couple of days afterward. You could see the dread on his face. James and Nate both had their heads back and eyes closed. Not Skylar, though. Skylar wanted to watch the beautiful Cambodian landscape disappear. He tried to take in every bit of the experience he had, knowing that his future was about to change drastically, and he most likely would never see this beloved place again.

The "wind-up plane," as Mark jokingly called it, began its ascent, and Skylar looked out the window at the villages he had called home for five months. He felt overwhelmed with emotion. He was sad to leave, excited to go home, but also scared to death!

As they rose above the clouds, the little plane lurched and rocked as it forged through the sky above the villages. Skylar rested his head against the window and watched the homes of the Khmer Loeu people disappear below him. As the plane went higher, he could see that the sky had turned abruptly from blue to gray, and he could also feel the change in the weather as the turbulence began to increase, bumping the plane along through black cloud formations.

Eventually, the ride started to feel like his four-wheeling adventures with his buddy Jack back home. They would take their ATVs down a bumpy gravel road behind Jack's grandpa's farm, and when they hit holes and ruts, their backsides completely lifted out of their seats. Skylar felt himself rising out of his chair on this ride too, but they were in the sky, not on a bumpy back road.

He looked up to see that Devin was clutching the arm of his chair with one hand and his barf bag with the other. Nate seemed to be sleeping, oblivious to the bumpy ride. James and Mark both had looks of concern written on their faces as well. Mark called up to Devin, "You okay, buddy?" Devin just nodded, looking straight ahead.

Their seats were directly behind the pilot in the small plane, and he continued to poke buttons and shift levers and move in ways that suggested he might be affected by the turbulence as well.

Skylar looked down at his watch and poked the light button on the side to check the time. His head popped back up quickly when a bolt of lightning seemed to shoot right through the plane. The noise was so loud and the light so bright that all five of the guys shouted with shock. It gave them a jolt, and the knot in Skylar's stomach began to tighten.

The sickening sounds of Devin heaving into his barf bag and the ensuing smell didn't help matters. The pilot had very broken English, and Skylar couldn't make out what he was saying into his headset. The tone of it, however, did not sound right. He realized the pilot was in a panic. He peered out his window but could see nothing but the driving, blowing sheets of rain pelting the little aircraft. Visibility was zero.

The tiny plane began to dip and dive and sway. At one point the aircraft dropped sideways so abruptly that Skylar's whole body fell against the wall, and he banged his head on the window. He felt sick and terrified, and by the looks on his friend's faces, they felt the same. By now, Nate had awakened from his deep sleep and was grabbing for his barf bag as well. Skylar tried to pray but felt so terrified all he could manage was "God help us!"

More lightning blazed outside the windows, and thunderclaps boomed through the cramped space. The pilot was visibly struggling to keep the aircraft under control. As the plane was buffeted in every direction, all five of them were grabbing their barf bags. Their bodies were moving, and they moaned and groaned as the plane would plunge and pivot.

The pilot cried, "Take position, take position!"

Mark shouted, "We're going to crash, guys, take the crash position!" All five of them bent forward to grab their knees and lower their heads.

"Pray, everyone! Pray!" Nate called out to them. Mark began to pray aloud in a muffled voice, the fear in his tone evident to all of them.

Skylar could not believe this was happening. *We are going to die. I'm never going to see Rae again.* A desperate prayer was all he could think of: "Oh mighty God, please help us!" By now the pilot had all but lost control of the plane, and he continued to shout, "Mayday, Mayday!" into his headset.

The plane dipped and plummeted, and Skylar braced himself for the impending crash. The cabin pressure dropped, and he felt as if his head would pop right off his shoulders. There was a pounding in his temples, and the sinking in his stomach intensified the agony. They were falling through the sky, spiraling downward, and there was nothing anyone could do. His worst nightmare was happening. Skylar and his buddies were falling to their death. He would never propose to Rae. He would never see his baby. Rae, his beautiful Rae, would raise their child alone.

"Oh, dear Father, help us!" Skylar cried out to God one last time.

CHAPTER
Seventeen

Mandy loved nothing more than to kick the shoes off her swollen feet after a day's work at the thrift store and walk barefoot through the soft soil of the garden. The seedlings were starting to peek up from the ground in neat little rows, and she couldn't wait to watch them grow and produce vegetables. Other than the windowsill gardens she helped plant in grade school, this was her first time taking part in the whole process, from sowing to reaping. She had been spending a lot of time there in the evenings at dusk, weeding and watering the garden. It was relaxing, and she enjoyed the serenity and quiet of it.

Mrs. B once said that the garden was her thinking spot, and Mandy could understand why. She was confident one could figure out any of the world's problems while in the garden. The garden— Mrs. B's whole backyard, for that matter—was tranquil and inviting. Mrs. B had worked diligently at making it a peaceful place with beautiful hanging baskets and urns of bright red geraniums. Mrs. B and Mandy had many meaningful conversations sitting on the stone patio under an archway of morning glories and ivy.

She loved this place and wished she would never have to leave. It felt like home. It wasn't just the garden or how neat and tidy Mrs. B kept the place. It wasn't the way the house always smelled of the fresh herbs growing in pots on the kitchen window sill or even the ever-present bouquet of flowers on the dining table. All those things added to the hominess for sure, but mostly it was how she felt when she was there.

Within these walls was a sense of belonging. Mandy had lived in a lot of places in her life. All of them had felt temporary. There was something about Mrs. B's home that felt just like home. Deep down, she knew it was Mrs. B's love and devotion to her that truly made it feel like home.

As hard as it would be to leave Mrs. B and this place, Mandy knew she couldn't keep imposing on her. She realized she would have to find somewhere else to live once her baby was born. She and Mrs. B hadn't talked about it much. It seemed that whenever she brought it up, Mrs. B quickly changed the subject, or something would distract them. Mrs. B didn't seem to be in a rush. In fact, Mandy felt that Mrs. B liked having her and Rae around. She was always making plans and spoiling them with new recipes and treats. Mandy wasn't complaining; she loved the attention for sure.

She wondered if maybe their presence in her home gave Mrs. B a sense of purpose. Mrs. B had spent years caring for her husband, followed by hard, lonely times after his death. Maybe caring for the girls filled some of the void she was experiencing. Mandy was sure that she would miss seeing Mrs. B daily when it was time for her to move. She was sure their friendship would continue, but Mandy was always comforted at the end of each day knowing she was going home to her. Sometimes she felt like a child going back to see her momma. And perhaps that was precisely how she was feeling; after all, going home to see her momma had always been a dream. With all the uncertainties that lay ahead of Mandy, the comfort of a mother was something she craved.

Mandy sadly recalled when she and her sisters had gone to their first foster home. Their foster mother, Mrs. Hancock, told the girls one Saturday evening about a week after their arrival that they were going to get cleaned up and their momma was coming to visit. Mrs. Hancock picked out those itchy church dresses for the girls again, and they proudly put them on. They wanted to look their finest for their momma. They sat in the parlor, and Mr. and Mrs. Hancock left the house after the social worker arrived. The social worker explained that she would be in the room while their momma was there, but they were to visit with her as they normally would and should just ignore her presence. She was charming, and the girls enjoyed chatting with her while waiting. They waited. They chatted. They waited some more.

Finally, Mr. and Mrs. Hancock arrived back home, and the social worker left. Before leaving she stooped down to their level and smiled sweetly at them, "I'm sorry, girls. Maybe your momma will show up for the next meeting." Mandy remembered the feeling of disappointment she felt. Krista cried big alligator tears, and Erin stomped off to her room. That was just one of the many times Mandy's mother disappointed her in life, but for some odd reason, Mandy always wanted to please her anyway.

"Mrs. B would never do that," Mandy thought out loud. Her feelings of sadness shifted to Mrs. B, as she was sure she would have been an excellent mother. It just didn't seem fair that her mother had three children that she barely cared for, and Mrs. B desperately wanted a child but couldn't have one.

Those kinds of situations were hard for Mandy to understand. Her old way of thinking would come back in those moments: thinking that life was unfair, that God wasn't fair. Fear, doubt, and lack of faith would creep into her mind. It was good to be studying, attending church, and learning the godly way of looking at these issues. There were so many things in life she didn't understand. Sometimes she wrote them down as they came to her so that she could ask Pastor or Mrs. B about them. The old Mandy would have just let them fester and grow into irreversible bitterness. The new

Mandy was learning that God was the healer of all wounds and had a purpose in all things.

Mandy swatted at a bee that hovered around her, interrupting her thoughts. "And I don't understand why God had to make you either!" she exclaimed out loud with a chuckle as she shooed it away.

"He made me to make delicious honey for bizzzz-kits!" Ayala said in her best bee voice. On her way out to the garden, she had heard Mandy fussing at the bee and decided to answer in the bee's stead.

Embarrassed that Mrs. B had caught her talking to a bee, but amused all the same, Mandy winked as she spoke, "Wow, I thought the bee was actually talking to me!"

"Well, I heard you questioning her existence and thought I would just be her voice," Ayala teased.

"Well, unfortunately for her, you're not a very good bee impersonator," Mandy quickly replied. Using air quotes, she continued, "You could 'bee' a lot better!"

"Hey, watch it. Haven't you heard?" Ayala asked.

"Heard what?" Mandy grinned expectantly.

"Haven't you heard that I'm what all the 'buzzzzzz' is about?" Ayala cracked up laughing at herself. Mandy couldn't help but laugh at her silliness also. "So what's up?" Ayala asked.

"Well, I was just weeding the garden and thinking about that big bowl of ice cream I'll have when I go in," Mandy said with a chuckle.

"Not until you finish your work, young lady," Ayala teased as she put her work gloves on and grabbed a bucket.

"Such a slave driver," Mandy mocked. The two were busy weeding and giggling when they heard a car pull in the drive.

Ayala kept packing soil around the bases of tomato plants as she spoke. "Hey, sounds like Rae is home. I hope she can relax tonight; that girl is running herself ragged. I'm worried about her."

"Yeah, she's working hard to keep her grades up," Mandy said matter-of-factly. "I think keeping the pregnancy a secret from her folks and waiting on Skylar to get home is just a lot of stress on her right now."

"Well, maybe she needs to get her toes in the dirt and have a little garden therapy," said Ayala. "I'll go get her."

Mandy couldn't resist one more opportunity to throw some silly sarcasm her way again, "Okay, you go ahead and do that," she said cheerily. "You know what they say? Age before beauty!" and now she laughed at herself.

Giggling, Mrs. B headed for the house, waddling, with her belly sticking out as if to mock Mandy.

Mandy yelled back at her with a laugh, "Well, you do make a better pregnant lady impersonator than a bee impersonator!"

CHAPTER

Eighteen

Rae was relieved to find no one in the house when she arrived. She needed a moment to figure out how she was going to approach Mandy with the article about her mother. While she was putting her things away in the bedroom, she heard Mrs. B call her from the mudroom.

"I'm in here—I'll be out in a minute," Rae replied.

Feeling tired, hungry, and frazzled, Rae didn't feel like facing anyone tonight. She wished she could just stay in her room and sleep until she heard from Skylar. She wondered where he was by now. It would be tomorrow until she heard from him, with the long travel and the time difference. She couldn't wait to see him, hug his neck, and hear all about his months away. She was thankful Skylar had seized such an awesome opportunity when he could. With what he was coming home to, he might never get another chance like this.

Rae couldn't help but feel anxious. She blamed a lot of it on her lack of sleep while cramming for finals, not to mention the conviction she was under for the lies and secrets that gnawed at her day and night. And now she had the added stress of figuring out how to approach Mandy about her mother's obituary. Her head was pounding with pain, to the extent that she was feeling nauseated. *Maybe I just need to have some dinner and hydrate*, she thought as she rubbed her temples.

She hoped Mrs. B was alone in the house. Maybe Rae could tell her about the article and get her advice on how to approach Mandy about her mother. She found Mrs. B in the mudroom, mixing up a blue fertilizer concoction for her roses on the patio.

"Hey, there's our hard-working girl!" Mrs. B greeted her with a grin.

"Well, I just hope all this hard work pays off," Rae said in a distracted tone.

"Rae, are you okay?" Mrs. B quizzed with concern in her eyes. "You look so tired and stressed." She took off her garden gloves and ran her hand down Rae's shoulder.

"Yes, I'm okay. It's just really a stressful time, and I came across something in the library that has me a little rattled. I saw it in the newspaper when I was researching—" The slamming screen door stopped Rae in mid-sentence.

"Hey, girls, did you leave a fat pregnant lady out here to do all the work herself?" Mandy interrupted as she bounded into the room.

"Well, somebody's gotta do the work, might as well be the fat pregnant gal," Rae teased as she poked her growing belly out in front of her and moved her hands for emphasis.

"Rae, why don't you grab something to eat and join us out in the garden?" Mrs. B offered. "It's a lovely evening!" She gave Rae a look that said, *we'll continue our conversation later*. She could tell that Rae's tone and facial expression had changed when Mandy came in, and she wondered if what she was about to say to her was private. She made a mental note to find time with her alone to see what was troubling her.

Mrs. B carried out her bucket of liquid fertilizer to the patio while Mandy rummaged through a drawer in the mudroom storage unit for more twine to use for the tomato stakes. Rae turned to the kitchen to see what she could find to eat. There was a pan of baked mac and cheese on the stovetop. Mrs. B was an excellent cook, and this looked creamy and delicious. She put a small portion in the microwave to heat up and poured herself a glass of cranberry juice. Mrs. B was adamant that the girls should have lots of vitamin C and had a variety of juices in the fridge. Rae wished she could take something for her headache, but she didn't want to do anything to put the baby in danger. She closed her eyes and rubbed her temples while she waited for the microwave timer to buzz.

When she closed her eyes, she could see Skylar, and she sighed a brief prayer for him that the Lord would bring him home safely. Lately, Rae's prayer life had also suffered. Short, on-the-fly prayers were all she could squeeze into her chaotic life. She took a deep breath and said "Amen." She grabbed a fork for her bowl of mac and cheese, picked up her drink, and headed out to the backyard. *Maybe some downtime with the girls will be a good way to de-stress a little,* she thought.

As she sat down on a deck chair, she felt her phone vibrate in her jeans pocket. She set her bowl aside and quickly pulled out the phone. *Could I be hearing from Skylar already?* she wondered. To her disappointment, the text was from her study partner, asking if Rae had heard back from the prof about a way to raise her grade. Rae had shared her plight with her friend, and it was sweet of her to inquire. Regretfully, she texted back, "Not yet." She hoped that on this subject, no news was good news. She would like to think the professor was working something up for her and was waiting to reply, but she feared that it wasn't likely.

Rae finally took a bite of mac and cheese. It tasted delicious, and she suddenly realized how hungry she was. Mrs. B and Mandy were now busy in the garden, tying up the tiny tomato plants with twine. Rae knew she should join them, but she had absolutely no desire to take part. She had never felt so exhausted in her life. Her head continued to pound, her feet were swollen and achy, and the weight of all her worries intensified everything. *No wonder my head hurts,* she thought to herself. *It's on overload.*

Mrs. B looked up from her work. "Have you heard anything from Skylar yet, Rae?"

"Not yet. I don't expect to hear anything until tomorrow maybe. I saw on the Facebook page that they were scheduled to leave the hill country this morning. I don't expect him to be able to contact me for some time, maybe not until he gets stateside."

"Oh Rae, I bet you're excited," Mandy called out from her garden spot.

Rae rose to approach the garden and continue the conversation. As soon as she was upright, however, she found herself grabbing for the archway to steady herself. Something didn't feel right. Rae could feel herself breaking into a sweat, the bite of mac and cheese stuck high in her stomach.

Mrs. B looked up to see Rae bracing herself and growing pale. "Rae, honey, are you okay?" She got up and began to remove her gloves.

"Yeah, I'm okay," Rae muttered. But clearly she wasn't, and she knew it. She was sure she was just exhausted and needed to take a nap. She didn't want Mrs. B and Mandy to know how little sleep she had been getting.

"I'm just really exhausted and have been fighting a headache all day." Forcing a grin, she went on, "I think I'll go nap for a little bit." She loosened her grip on the archway and headed for the house, eager to lie down and try to feel better. She took one step. Her feet felt heavy, and the ground suddenly seemed very close. The patio was spinning, and everything grew dark. She frantically reached for the arch to support her as she was going down.

Mrs. B could see what was happening and began to sprint toward her. She couldn't get there fast enough. Rae went down with a thud on the patio; the glass dish in her hand hit the ground and spread shattered glass all around her.

Mandy was still looking down, but the sound of the crashing dish startled her, and she gasped. *"Rae!"* Mandy screamed at the sight of her fallen friend.

"Oh, my sweet Rae!" Mrs. B knelt next to her. "Mandy, call 911, quick!" Mandy grabbed the phone from her pocket and frantically dialed.

Assessing Rae's condition, Mrs. B slid her finger under her wrist. Rae didn't respond to her touch, but she was breathing, and her pulse seemed okay. She cradled Rae's head in her lap and called out to Mandy to get a wet cloth for her forehead, and Mandy obliged. She grabbed a broom on the way out to sweep up the broken glass and was just discarding it when the ambulance arrived.

Mandy and Mrs. B stood arm in arm as they watched the ambulance leave with their sweet friend Rae. They both pleaded to God to help their friend and her baby.

CHAPTER
Nineteen

"Mister! Mister! You go now, mister!"

Skylar heard a voice and felt someone shaking his shoulder, but he couldn't quite seem to wake up. "Did we crash? Am I dead?" he mumbled in his confused, sleepy state.

"Mister, you wake up now. We land safely. Mister, mister!"

Skylar finally managed to open his eyes. He was peering into the face of the disheveled, wide-eyed pilot. Skylar tried to gather his wits and make sense of where he was and what was going on.

"Hey, mister – you go now. New plane come for you," the pilot spoke in broken English.

"What? What's going on? Did we crash? Where are we?" Skylar asked, straightening in his seat and looking around. "Where are my friends? Are they okay?" His panic grew as he began to remember what was happening before he blacked out, sure they were doomed, never to wake up on this side of heaven again.

"Your friends outside, wait for new plane," the pilot said as he tugged on Skylar's arm to try to get him moving.

He slowly unsnapped his seat belt. "But did we crash? What is going on?" His whole body ached, and he moaned a little as he moved forward.

"No, I good pilot—I land plane," the pilot said with a gap-toothed grin.

Skylar grabbed his scattered belongings and stood up. When he did, he realized that he felt like he had been in a crash. Every part of his body ached. As he walked toward the front exit, he could see the pilot's oxygen mask dangling from the ceiling. He pointed to it and looked back at the pilot. "Did we all have oxygen masks?"

"No, just me. I need it most" was the matter-of-fact reply.

"Well, I'm glad you did, and hey, thanks for landing us safely," Skylar said, offering his hand.

Once outside, Skylar found his friends sitting in a row as if they were lined up in a firing range. They all had a stunned look.

Skylar took a seat on the ground next to his friend Mark. "What in the world is going on, Mark? How did we not crash? I mean, was I the only one who blacked out? I don't remember anything except the plane dropping!"

Mark mirrored Skylar's expression of shock and amazement. "I don't know, dude. The pilot just got us out, like he did you, and told us we have to wait on another plane. All I can make of it is that we all blacked out due to lack of oxygen. Apparently, he had an oxygen mask and somehow was able to get the plane straightened out and landed in this field.

"I have no idea where we are, dude. I just know that was the scariest thing I have ever been through in my life, and the idea of getting on another plane does not sound good at all!"

Skylar was surprised to hear this from his fearless friend, who always exuded confidence in tight situations. He had never seen Mark so rattled. He understood, as he himself was still shaken. He wondered how Devin was doing; he'd been afraid of the flight from the minute they stepped on. As he looked down the row of his friends seated on the ground, it was undeniable that poor Devin was taking it the hardest of them all. He hugged his knees to himself and rocked back and forth on the ground. All five of the guys sat in the grass in the field looking shocked and dumbfounded as they waited for instruction.

Skylar bowed his head now, and tears rolled down his cheeks again. He hated to cry in front of his friends, who were trying to be brave, but he was incredibly thankful to be alive. He patted his shirt pocket to make sure the bamboo pouch and ring were still there. When he felt the little lump in his pocket, he let his hand linger there for a moment, as if he was touching Rae herself. Just less than an hour earlier he thought he'd never see her again, and now he had been given a second chance. Skylar couldn't believe he was alive; he'd been sure the flight was doomed as they fell. He was thankful he had blacked out. He was sure it was God's way of protecting him and his friends from the harrowing landing that must have taken place. By the looks of the plane, he was sure the landing had not been smooth.

Skylar prayed silently but was moved to embrace his friends and pray a prayer of thanksgiving to God for His mighty protection over them. He arose and knelt behind them and extended his arms to cover all of them and began to pray. He could feel both Nate and James shaking with emotion. Mark agreed with him in prayer as he whispered, "Thank You, Jesus," throughout the prayer. Devin however, continued to hug his knees, rocking back and forth.

After Skylar said amen, he got close to Devin and put his hands on his shoulders. "How ya doin', buddy?" There was no reply; Devin looked straight ahead and rocked back and forth. Skylar looked over at his friends with concern on his face, "Hey, guys, you think Devin is okay?" Each of them took turns talking to him, getting in his face and trying to rouse some reaction or eye contact, but there was nothing. It was painfully clear to all of them, Devin was in a state of shock.

The pilot was unloading his personal belongings and fussing over the plane. When he landed, the propeller must have hit the ground in the soft soil, as the aircraft looked to be stuck. As Skylar looked at it, he wondered how in the world the pilot did manage to land the plane in such an odd place. He could see there was a swatch cut out of the field where the plane came in, but he just couldn't understand how it had come to a stop, or how he got it straightened out. Mostly, he wondered how they were going to get out of there and how they were to take another plane. There did not appear to be room for another plane.

Skylar walked over to the pilot. "It's a miracle you landed this thing," he said.

"I good pilot, I always land plane," the pilot insisted.

"My buddies and I were just thanking God for your skill and for His protection of you and the plane. Dude, I mean, I thought we were goners!" Skylar said as he shook his head and raked his fingers over his disheveled hair.

"Bad storm, but not worst I see. I always land, I land all places," he said with an air of cockiness.

It may have been an incredibly confident statement, and this man definitely claimed the victory as his own, but Skylar didn't care. He thought this man's overconfidence had paid off here for sure. "What now?" he asked the pilot. "Do we need to walk somewhere?"

"Copter come for you"—he held up two fingers—"two at a time."

"Oh, so, we will take a helicopter from here, two at a time?"

"We wait for copter."

"Well, my friend over there, the one rocking back and forth, well, umm, I think he might be in shock or something. I think he might need to see a doctor. Is there a way to get him to a doctor?" Skylar looked around at his surroundings knowing good and well that there was no doctor around, but he was hoping the pilot would suggest a way of getting Devin some help.

"No doctor, we wait on copter. He know," the pilot said with a nod as if the helicopter pilot might moonlight as a physician or something.

"Okay, do you have any idea how long it will take for the

helicopter to come? We have to catch other flights today." Skylar said, hoping fervently the pilot would say the "copter" was on its way.

"Copter come later when free. He make deliveries first, then he come for us."

Skylar nodded with disappointment. He had no idea what that could mean and how long they might sit in this field before any of them reached the next leg of the journey. To make matters worse, he was concerned that Devin might need some medical help. He wished their instructor was with them right now, but he had stayed back to visit with friends he had gotten to know over the years of taking part in the program.

Skylar reported what little he knew to the guys, and they continued to talk to Devin and try to get him to drink from the water bottles they had taken aboard. Still no response from Devin. Nothing, except the glazed stare and the rocking motion. The sun mounted steadily higher in the sky, and the wait for the helicopter seemed to take forever. Occasionally, the pilot spoke to them, but for the most part he kept to himself. They had eaten all the snacks they had brought with them and rationed out their water supply.

Even though none of them were too excited about flying again, they were anxious to move forward on their journey. At this point, the men had no idea if they would make their connections or when they'd be home. They talked about how the program director at the university was keeping track of their flights and was posting to the program's Facebook page when flights were leaving and arriving so that eager family members could keep up with their progress. When he didn't receive flight confirmation of this trip, he might get worried, as would their families.

Noon turned into dusk and hunger pangs set in for all of them. The concern for Devin grew stronger as they were unable to get him to drink or eat anything, and they feared he would get dehydrated. They had moved him to the shade of a nearby tree, but he immediately went back into shock mode. He had stopped rocking, but now he sat with his back against the tree, just staring ahead. Mark volunteered to accompany Devin on the first flight, and he would try to seek medical treatment for him somehow. Mark had traveled a lot with his military family over the years and wasn't afraid to tackle airports in foreign cities by himself. He was happy to stay with Devin, as long as he needed him.

At last, in the distance, they could hear the distinct whopping of helicopter blades. The pilot had them all move away from the clearing. He began to wave a white flag from his emergency kit on the plane, and the helicopter came in for a landing. A crew member got off to assess the situation and help passengers on board. He seemed to have better English than the pilot, and Mark explained Devin's situation to him. The crewman agreed that he needed some medical attention. He decided to fly the two of them to a hospital near Phnom Penh International Airport. Since this would take some time, he also agreed to call for another helicopter to come for the remainder of the group.

Skylar was relieved to hear that he would not have to wait out this helicopter's round trip. But he still would be waiting. He had no other choice. He had to be patient and just trust that God would get them all safely to the airport, work out the details of their connections (which they had long since missed already), and pray that their families weren't worried sick about them.

But mostly, he prayed that his friend Devin would be okay.

CHAPTER
Twenty

Ayala grabbed Rae's backpack from her room before she and Mandy headed to the hospital. She was scolding herself for not taking the time to get emergency numbers from the girls in case something like this happened. Now here she was, not knowing how to get in touch with Rae's folks, not knowing about her insurance or medical history. Since Rae was twenty-one years old, out of respect for her as an adult she had never asked for that sort of information. She regretted that decision now.

She wasn't sure whether to call Rae's parents. They were so close to having Skylar home, and her plans of telling her parents about the baby with him were about to unfold. Ayala didn't want to ruin that for her, but if Rae or the baby was truly in danger, she felt Rae's parents should know. Determined she would have a better grip on this once they got to the hospital, Ayala pushed the accelerator, anxious to get there.

Mandy sat in the passenger's seat rifling through Rae's messy backpack.

"Wow," she exclaimed. "She sure has a lot of stuff in here!"

The paramedic had taken Rae's phone out of her pocket and handed it to Mandy before they took her in the ambulance. She could see that the battery was low, so she paused her backpack search long enough to plug it into the car charger. The phone was no good to them without the passcode, but they took it anyway in case Rae needed it.

Mandy was shaking with worry for her friend. She was worried about what might happen to the baby if she gave birth at this point. Maybe she was just exhausted and needing rest, she thought, trying to stay positive. She prayed silently that whatever was going on would involve a simple fix.

At last, she found Rae's wallet in the confines of the bag and began to search through it for insurance cards or anything that might be helpful at the hospital. She came across her ID and an insurance card. She knew Rae had been paying her doctor's visits out of pocket at the clinic because she didn't want it going through the insurance for her dad to see. Mandy didn't know if this insurance card was valid or not. She pulled out her ID, and behind it was an "In Case of Emergency" card.

"Oh look," she exclaimed. "Here's emergency numbers in her wallet with her dad's phone number in case we need it."

"Great," said Ayala, "I just wish I had clear direction on what to do about that. Hopefully, once we're there, we'll get a handle on whether to call her parents or not."

"Oh, this stinks! She is so close to having Skylar home and telling her parents about the baby." Mandy shoved Rae's wallet into her bag and let out a sigh of discouragement. She heard a ting on Rae's phone. She picked it up to see who it was. It was Rae's dad. He was asking if she had heard from Skylar yet.

"This is good," Ayala said, "We can slide that over and reply to it and text him if we need to without putting her passcode in, right?"

Mandy nodded. "Yes, that's right … we can do that on her

smartphone, I believe. But I'm praying Rae can make this call herself."

Ayala zoomed into the Mercy Hospital parking lot. She hated this place. She got a sinking feeling every time she drove by it. In this building her beloved Tim had taken his last breath. Ayala had vowed when she left that day that she would never step foot in Mercy Hospital again. The smell of the place dredged up painful memories of the days and nights spent by Tim's bedside, praying and begging for a miracle. Ayala knew she had to be brave for Rae, however, and put all those feelings aside. After all, she was carrying out the work Tim had encouraged her to do, and she wanted to honor that.

She hooked her arm into Mandy's, and they headed inside toward the emergency room. "We're here for Rae Carver," Ayala told the clerk at the nurse's station.

"Are you family?" she asked, peering over the top of her glasses.

"Well, we are the only family she has here. Her family is in Minnesota. She lives with us here while she's in college." She was prepared to beg and plead with the woman.

"I'm sorry, but we would have to get her permission to let you come in. I'll get your names, and you can have a seat in the lobby," she said with a click of her pen.

They gave the clerk their names and took a seat. Worry set in, and they were anxious to get an update. Ayala began to pace and then went back to the window, hoping to reason with the woman at the desk.

"I understand your policy, but you see, her parents don't know she's pregnant. She's waiting until her boyfriend returns from a study trip, which is now, I mean, it's happening right now. He's flying home today, is what I'm trying to say, and she should be hearing back from him soon"

Ayala was visibly shaken and stammering. "I mean, we are all she has right now. If there is something serious going on, would you please let me know so I can contact her parents? I just feel bad that she's all alone," she added, struggling to put an end to her own rambling.

The clerk could see the concern through Ayala's awkwardness. "I know you're worried. I must follow government rules and regulations for hospitals. The doctor is in with her now. I'll go back and speak to her soon and let her know you are here." The clerk seemed to be softening to Ayala's desperation.

Ayala went back to sit by Mandy even though it was tough to sit still. She was regretting that she didn't push Rae to tell her parents about the pregnancy, and it showed in her restlessness.

"Stop beating yourself up over this, Mrs. B," Mandy admonished. "Rae is an adult, and she has had good reason not to tell her folks yet. You and I both know she is going to. You haven't done anything wrong." She laid her hand on Ayala's shoulder. "You know, someone much wiser than myself once told me that I need to 'let go and let God take care of the situation.'" She gave her wise friend a nod.

"You're right, Mandy—I guess your friend is pretty wise after all," Ayala teased. She certainly wasn't feeling wise at the moment. With a glance back toward the registration window, she said, "I hope they will give us an update at least."

Back in the examination room, Rae was riddled with guilt. She couldn't believe she had awakened in the back of an ambulance and was now in the hospital hooked up to whirring machines, a blood pressure cuff that squeezed her arm automatically every few minutes, and a host of people throwing questions at her. "Your sins will find you out," Rae muttered under her breath. "I've said so many lies, kept so many secrets, denied my body all the things it needs to get my grades up, and now it's all catching up with me. And my baby is suffering because of it. I must be the worst mother in the world." She broke into sobs.

The nurse who checked on Rae could see that she was upset. Knowing this could elevate her blood pressure even more, she told her about the women in the lobby, hoping it would settle her nerves a bit. "I can send one of them back to be with you if you want," she offered, "but I can't have them both back here."

"Yes, please send Mrs. Banks back," Rae said with a sniff. The nurse made some notations on Rae's chart and headed to the lobby.

"Mrs. Banks," the nurse called from the ER door. Ayala stood up quickly and almost sprinted to the door with Mandy right behind her.

"I'm sorry, I can only let one of you back in the room, but Rae is requesting a Mrs. Banks."

Ayala and Mandy locked eyes. Mandy squeezed Ayala's arm. "It's okay, Mrs. B, I'll be fine out here. Just let me know what's going on, please!" Ayala promised to do so and followed the nurse back to the room where Rae lay crying in her bed.

"Rae—oh, honey, it's so good to see you're okay. Don't cry; it's going to be okay," Mrs. B crooned as she leaned over Rae and stroked her red wavy mane.

"Mrs. B, this is all my fault. I'm a terrible mom. I haven't taken care of myself, and my baby could pay for it. My grades and telling lies and keeping secrets from my parents have all caught up with me. I've put all this stuff ahead of my baby. I just feel awful."

At this, Rae frantically waved toward the bedside pan. Ayala handed it to her quickly, and Rae vomited into it. Ayala rang for the nurse and continued to fuss over Rae, stroking her hair, wiping her tears, and assuring her that it was all going to be okay.

"Rae, honey, don't you think we need to call your parents and let them know you're here? Don't you want them here with you right now?"

"No, no, not yet. Skylar is so close to being home. —My phone, where's my phone?" Rae cried out in a panic. "He may be trying to call me, and if I'm not there to pick it up, he will worry!"

"Shh, shh, Rae. Don't worry; Mandy has your phone. She will keep guard over it. If he tries to call or texts, she'll answer or let us know. There are restrictions on phones back here in the exam rooms."

"Oh please, Mrs. B, please tell Mandy to respond if Skylar calls or texts and let him know I'm in the hospital and I need him!" Fresh tears overflowed.

In her years caring for Tim, Ayala had learned a thing or two about reading hospital monitors. She could see by the monitor attached to Rae's blood pressure cuff that all this panic and fretting was not helping her at all. She also knew from her training at the Center for Hope that high blood pressure and pregnancy didn't mix.

"Rae, listen to me. You must get ahold of yourself! If you want to take care of your baby, you must try to calm down and get your blood pressure down. I know your world seems out of control right now, but you must remember that God's got this: *He* is in control. None of this is bigger than He is. Now, I want you to lay back and close your eyes and take in some deep breaths!" Ayala didn't want to scare her, but she wanted her to understand the importance of calming down.

"When the doctor comes back with all your test results, we will have a better grasp of what's going on, and then we will make the decision, together, whether or not your parents need to be informed before Skylar gets in." Ayala stroked the top of Rae's hand. She hated to be so firm with her, but she felt that someone had to be a voice of reason for her right now.

With Rae's hand in her own, Ayala began to pray over her. As she prayed, she could feel Rae relaxing, her deep breaths were becoming less intentional and more natural. Before she knew it, Rae had fallen asleep. She was sure it was from pure exhaustion.

CHAPTER
Twenty One

Skylar breathed a sigh of relief as he clicked his seat belt shut on his flight to Hong Kong. He was finally on his way. He thought he would feel more apprehensive about flying after his harrowing ordeal, but his urgency to get home and figure out his future made him more eager than afraid to get in the air.

He could see the back of James's and Nate's heads from his seat. Having missed their original flight, they were able to get on this plane entirely by a miracle. When the man at the ticket counter told them there were three available seats, Skylar knew those three spots were a gift from God. He was sad that Mark and Devin weren't flying with them but was relieved to find out from the helicopter pilot who came for them that Devin would stay at the hospital for observation, and the two would fly out the next day. Skylar was thankful for his friend Mark and gleaned much from his godly witness while they were away. It was very in line with Mark's character to make this sacrifice for Devin and wait a day.

The university program Facebook manager was supposed to update the page when their flights left from each hub. Skylar was guessing he had no way of knowing the team hadn't made the flights and were running behind. Rae and his family were probably awaiting a call from him at any time, but that just wasn't going to happen.

Skylar had decided he would charge his phone at their layover in Hong Kong and try to find a computer station where he could access his Facebook account and update everyone on their progress. It had been a long day, and he was exhausted. Once the plane was up in the air and the drink cart came by, Skylar ate the bagged lunch he was given and drank a can of soda as quickly as he could. He realized then just how famished he was. They were so rushed getting through Phnom Penh airport, they had no time to take care of necessities.

Skylar adjusted his position in the seat and sat back for the long flight. Maybe this would be a good time to catch up on much-needed sleep, he thought as he closed his eyes. But his mind would not let him rest. Even though he and Rae had originally made plans for him to drive to Indiana to pick her up in a week, he wondered if he could wait that long. There was a lot to do when he got back home. He had to finish up his thesis paper from all his research, something he had been working on for weeks. He was making progress with the assignment, but it was all handwritten because of his primitive conditions in the hill country. Once home, he would have to type it and add the finishing touches.

Since it was a senior thesis, the study abroad program had allowed him a lot of time to complete it before he graduated. Skylar wanted to get it done as quickly as possible, however, while everything was still fresh in his mind and before he could be diverted by the tangled mass of issues that lay ahead of him.

He hoped to work on it as much as possible during the next week before he went to get Rae. He understood that she would need a lot of his attention, as she had been going it alone all these months without him, and he wanted to give her as much support as he could. A *feeble attempt of making up for lost time, perhaps,* he thought. He also wanted to marry her as soon as they could get a license. He reached up and touched the lump in his shirt pocket again; his heart skipped a beat at the thought of finally making Rae his wife.

The mere thought of getting married was hard to grasp, but the idea of them being parents was utterly beyond his reach. He could not even imagine Rae being pregnant and giving birth or the two of them getting up in the night to console a newborn baby. Buying diapers, figuring out child care, how to make it financially, where they were going to live … his list of worries grew with each mile. Thinking about how his life was changing made him dizzy. He just needed more time for all of this to sink in. *I'm sure reality will sink in when I can see it with my own eyes,* he thought.

Skylar hadn't given much thought to how he was going to tell his parents. Now the prospect was spinning around in his brain and chasing away his sleep. His parents loved Rae and fully expected the two of them to be married someday. In fact, they'd be more upset, most likely, if he told them he'd broken up with Rae. He didn't worry so much about them being upset about a grandbaby; he guessed his mom would be thrilled.

He did worry, though, about their disappointment that he and Rae broke their vows of purity before marriage with each other. His dad and Rae's dad were both respectable servants in their church. What shame and embarrassment they would cause both of their parents and their church families. The thought made Skylar sick to his stomach. Admittedly, he had let them all down, and he and Rae would have a hard time facing any of them.

Skylar's mind traveled back to a couple of summers ago when he and Rae were counselors at Camp Ravenswood. They sat around the campfire with a group of youth and talked to them about abstinence and staying pure. They gave examples of how they resisted temptation in their relationship. He had prayed for several dating couples around the fire that they would stay pure. *What a hypocrite I am to them,* he thought. *I can't even practice what I preach!*

Skylar had learned a great deal about himself on his trip. He was convicted by the simplicities of life and how entitled and spoiled he had been. Before he had learned about Rae's pregnancy, he'd felt sure God was calling him to missions. That whole idea had now been shoved to the back of Skyler's mind. He was resigned to the fact that God would never call someone who couldn't even set a solid example for youth. Could a man whose wife had been pregnant when they got married be trusted to give anyone's children godly counsel? Shame and embarrassment choked out his last hope of mission work.

He could only imagine how ashamed Rae must feel. The famous words she often quoted, "Your sins will find you out," echoed in Skylar's mind. *We sinned, and now we're paying for it with a baby!* The thought instantly burned a hole right through his soul. As soon as he thought it, he wished he could take it back. "God," he prayed, "what kind of horrible tyrant have I become that I would think of my child, this amazing miracle of Your design, as a punishment? Dear Lord, please forgive me!" Shame overcame him as he prayed, and he could not stop the flow of tears.

This baby is a miracle. All life is a miracle, a precious gift from God, created by Him with purpose. God already knows the numbers of hair on my baby's head. He has plans already in motion for him or her, and now Skylar was remorseful for even thinking of this precious life as a punishment for a weak moment he and Rae had encountered.

This baby was a blessing. He had been too self-centered and focused on how parenthood was going to ruin his plans instead of recognizing how it most likely would enrich his life in ways he couldn't even fathom. Skylar shook his head at how selfish he had become. All he could think about was himself and how this baby would change the course of his plans.

Then Skylar felt God's peace engulf him. His fear began to dissipate, and hope started to filter into his heart. He was reminded of God's truth from Isaiah 55:8–9: "My thoughts are not your thoughts, neither are your ways My ways, declares the LORD. As the heavens are higher than the earth, so are My ways higher than your ways and My thoughts than your thoughts."

Skylar wiped the tears from his eyes, as fresh, new ones fell into his lap. These tears, though, weren't falling because of shame and shattered dreams as before; these tears flowed out of renewed thankfulness and hope.

CHAPTER
Twenty Two

Mandy sipped the soda she had purchased from the machine outside the waiting room. "What is taking so long?" she muttered impatiently. It seemed hours had passed since Mrs. B was called back to the examining room to see Rae.

She felt a little kick in her abdomen as she tried to make herself comfortable in the hard chair. "Oh no, little one, it's not the time to play!" she whispered. She ran her hand along her rounded belly to see if her baby girl would kick back at her touch; this was the game they played together lately. She let out a little giggle when her baby girl obliged and gave her hand a hard thump. She was glad she was the only one in the waiting room, as anyone watching would surely think she was crazy.

She was incredibly bored and scanned the magazine rack for something to occupy her time. She skimmed over the publications, but when her hand grazed over a *Seek and Find* puzzle book, she was quick to snatch it up, forgetting there was no one in the room to fight her for it. It was probably just instinct for her. She remembered that she and her sisters used to have a book much like this one when they were young. Their mother had purchased it to keep them occupied when she did laundry at a local laundromat. The book kept her and her sisters entertained for hours. The sisters would fight over the book quite often but usually resolved to work on the puzzle together, with all three of them hovering over the small page pointing out words for one another to circle.

Now if only I had a pen or pencil, Mandy thought as she surveyed the room in hopes of seeing one. Her eye went to Rae's backpack. *Well, surely that messy bag has a pen in it somewhere ... if I dare to venture into no-man's-land.* She snickered, imagining her friend would find the humor in her statement if she were there.

Mandy looked through the front pockets, as this seemed a logical place to keep writing tools. But since she was dealing with her "illogical" friend's backpack; there was no such luck. She unzipped the main pocket and began to pull out its contents, looking for a pen or pencil in the dark confines. A folder, a notebook, a weathered and worn map of the campus, two granola bar wrappers, and a newspaper later... she found a pen. She stuck the pen behind her ear and started to put everything back in the bag but decided that the notebook and newspaper stacked up on top of her big belly would make a great desk on which to work.

She opened the puzzle book to the next available page, folded back the cover, and began her search. The first two words she found rather quickly, so she scanned her eyes up to the top of the page to look at the word list. When she did, a name jumped out at her from the newspaper obituary index nestled next to her book. *Patrice Lewis*. Mandy stared at it. It had been a long time since she had seen or heard the name, Patrice Lewis. Now it stared her in the face—in the obituary section no less.

Mandy put her puzzle book down and thumbed through the newspaper until she found the obituary:

Patrice Lewis, 44, who resided at Southside
Mission House, was found dead on Tuesday
morning at the corner of Market and 4th Street of
an apparent overdose. Arrangements are pending
with Gutherman Funeral Home. (See "Homeless
Woman identified"—cover page)

Mandy closed the paper quickly and scanned the front page
for the article. And there it was: an article about her mother dying
as a homeless woman on a street corner. The report referred to
her mother as a "bag lady." She was found lying in a heap with no
identification. The article mentioned that authorities were looking
for relatives.

For what? Mandy wondered. *Do they want someone to pay for
her burial?*

Mandy grew numb. She had no idea how to feel about what
she had just read. The only emotion she could muster was shame—
shame that she didn't feel anything, shame that she didn't feel sad
or sorry or empathetic toward her mother. She felt shame that her
mother died because of selfishness, her need for a fix, which had
always been more significant than anything else in her life.

Mandy dropped the paper and stared blankly into space. Her
mother had already been dead to her for many years. She didn't
understand why she felt any emotion, even at realizing that the
possibility of ever reconciling with her was now completely gone. It
wasn't as if she thought it ever would have happened, but there was
always a smidgen of hope that it might someday.

Even with the odds stacked against her; she never gave up
on having a "real" family. Over the last several months she had
experienced the joy of forgiveness and was learning how to forgive
others. Secretly, she had hoped to experience healing in her
relationship with her mother and be able to forgive her.

She looked around the empty ER room. Once again, Mandy
Lewis felt abandoned and alone. And there it was, that sick, sinking

feeling in her stomach. The same feeling she had as a child, every time her mother left her and her sisters to fend for themselves.

Mrs. B's voice from the ER door was like salve to her wounded soul, and Mandy was relieved to see her for many reasons. She threw the newspaper and books down into the chair next to her and stood up to meet Mrs. B. "What's going on with Rae?"

"Well, the doctor said her blood pressure is high, but they don't feel she has preeclampsia—at least, not yet. She also has a urinary tract infection and is somewhat dehydrated. And she had low blood sugar when she came in. They're giving her an IV and monitoring her overnight." Ayala sighed with relief.

"And the baby checks out okay?" Mandy asked.

"Yes, I got to hear the heartbeat, and it's strong and sweet!" Mrs. B said proudly. "But they are keeping the monitors in place as well overnight. Just as a precaution."

"Oh that's wonderful news!"

"Mandy, I feel like I should stay here overnight with her. She's struggling with all of this and feeling a lot of guilt—blaming herself for everything." She looked Mandy in the eye. "Are you okay staying home alone?"

"Yes, Mrs. B, I think that is a great idea. I'll keep the home fires burning. By the way, I checked Rae's phone earlier just to see if anything had come in from Skylar or her parents. There was nothing, but she was almost out of power. I'm sure it's dead by now or going to be soon. Should I just take it home and charge it up?"

"Oh boy, I don't know. She's very anxious about that phone and being able to get word from Skylar. Since I have to go home and grab a few things for the night, why don't we just grab her charger and bring it back with me?"

"Good idea. Do you think I can go back and see her?"

"Sure, I don't see why not. They're just waiting to take her upstairs."

Mandy returned Rae's items to her backpack, tucked the puzzle book away on the rack, and headed toward the ER desk to get permission to go back. She had already decided she wouldn't bring up this situation with her mom until things with Rae were more settled. Rae and Mrs. B were Mandy's family now, and Rae's health was top priority.

CHAPTER
Twenty Three

Skylar told Nate and James about his plan to post to the Study Abroad Facebook page after they landed. Then he headed out to find a charging station for his phone. Once he got the phone hooked in and the Wi-Fi turned on, he logged onto his Facebook account. He was able to access the Study Abroad page and post a quick note to it:

"An update from Hong Kong Airport. We experienced a delay in our first flight and didn't make our second one. We just now arrived in Hong Kong. Mark and Devin will be on a flight in the morning, so their arrival is undetermined. We are all doing well and anxious to get back home. Nate, James, and I will leave from Hong Kong in about two hours. Our flight schedule is messed up, and we have several stops along the way. We will update when we can."

The charging station was full now, and a man stood impatiently waiting for his turn at the outlets. Skylar ignored him and continued his Facebook search. He hit the post button and then quickly typed in Rae's name at the top. Her beautiful face on the screen was a sight for sore eyes. Even though he took pictures of her with him to Cambodia, this recent profile picture made his heartbeat speed up a bit. She was stunning; she always had been. But there was something about this photo; she seemed to have a glow about her he'd never seen before. *Apparently motherhood suits my honey*, he thought proudly.

He was sure she was anxiously waiting to hear from him; so he clicked the message button and hoped he'd be able to enter into a conversation with her.

"Rae, I'm in Hong Kong finally. I'm looking at 20 or more hours of travel time before I get into Minneapolis. I hope you get this message and we can chat a bit before my flight leaves. Hello? Hello?"

Skylar stared at the screen, hoping to get a reply. He desperately wanted to hear from Rae. Soon, a balloon of dots popped up on the screen signifying the other party was typing a message. He could hardly contain his excitement.

"Hi, Skylar, this is Mandy. I am Rae's friend. Unfortunately, Rae wasn't feeling well and is in the hospital. She is okay but staying overnight for observation. I am charging her phone for her and wanted to reply to you to let you know what's going on and that she is very anxious to hear from you. She lives with me and a wonderful woman by the name of Ayala Banks who has opened her home to us. Mrs. Banks is going to stay with her at the hospital. She will give Rae her phone if you have time to check back later."

Skylar couldn't believe what he was reading. He grazed his finger over the screen to reply as he ignored the annoying foot tapping of the man waiting in line.

"What? Is she okay? What's going on? Why did she go to the hospital? Is the baby okay? Do her parents know?"

Skylar's heart felt as if it might pound right out of his chest. He had endless questions and was trying desperately to get as much info out of Mandy as he could.

"Lots of stress … trying to keep her grades up, hiding everything from her parents, etc. She passed out, and we called an ambulance. Lack of sleep and nutrition. Blood pressure is high, blood sugar low, dehydrated and has a little infection. Doc not too concerned about her BP yet. She's on IV and resting. Parents don't know ... waiting on you. Baby checks out fine."

Skylar instantly felt guilty. He felt sorry that he had put Rae in this position. He wasn't surprised that she would work herself into a frenzy to keep up her grades and try to juggle everything. But she just had to take care of herself, and he was going to make sure that she did from now on. He couldn't get there fast enough.

"Please tell her to message me when she can, and I will respond as soon as I'm able to. Please tell her I love her!"

"Will do, Skylar. Please don't worry—she is in good hands. I'm sorry you had to find out this way but felt you should know."

"I'm so glad you told me. Thank you."

With his phone adequately charged and only an hour to get a bite to eat, he gathered his things and set out to find his friends and continue his journey home. He wished now that he was going to Indianapolis instead of Minneapolis. Skylar needed to get to Rae and his baby as soon as he could. Now he had extra worry to add to his list.

He grabbed a drink and a sandwich at a deli and headed toward his terminal. He spotted Nate and James right away. They looked tired and weary. They asked him if he had updated the Facebook page. Skylar nodded, the stress of what had just transpired with Mandy showing on his face. His friends recognized he was troubled.

"Something wrong, man?" Nate asked.

"Yeah, dude, you look like you just lost your best friend or something," James added.

He'd kept the news of Rae's pregnancy to himself the last two weeks, so his friends had no idea what he was up against once he got home. Now, with this new information, he felt like he had a mass of tangled wires in his brain all short-circuiting. He certainly felt stressed; no wonder his friends were asking. The stress was all-consuming; he couldn't contain it any longer.

He had spent many nights around the campfire talking and sharing laughs with these two guys over the last few months, maybe he should confide in them now. He trusted that Nate and James would keep his confidence and maybe give him some much-needed advice; even if they only served as a sounding board, he needed to talk through all of this before he went crazy. He decided to divulge his secret and express his worries to his two friends.

"Well, it does have to do with my best friend," he began. "My Rae."

"Oh yeah—little Red?" James said jokingly. He always teased Skylar about his fiery red-headed girlfriend. He grew serious when he saw that Skylar didn't crack a smile. "What's going on? Are you guys okay?"

"Well, not exactly." Skylar sighed. "You see, Rae and I have known each other our whole lives. She's the only girl I've ever dated, the only one I ever wanted to. We decided years ago that we wanted to 'wait' until our wedding day." His air quotes meant to emphasize what the word *wait* meant. Nate and James nodded to show they understood.

"Let me tell you; it hasn't been easy. I mean, you've seen her, right?" A prideful grin graced his lips for a second to lighten the mood a little before he broke his life-altering news. "I mean, we did good, ya know ... until right before our trip. We were alone together over Thanksgiving break, and we broke our vow to each other. I guess we just got caught up in the heat of the moment. We both knew we shouldn't have. We felt terrible afterward. We both prayed for forgiveness and swore it wouldn't happen again. When I left, I felt like we were back on track ... with God and each other."

Nate and James pulled in closer to Skylar as his voice started to trail and fill with emotion.

"A couple of weeks ago when we went into the city, I accessed a public computer site and got onto Facebook for a few minutes. Rae had left me a private message some time ago that she is pregnant! I just can't believe it. I've been trying to process it for a couple of weeks now, and I feel like we need to get married as soon as possible, and then maybe after the baby comes we can have a real wedding."

"Hey, congrats, man!" James said with a big grin, trying to hide his shock. "You're gonna be a papa, dude; that's awesome!"

Nate chimed in, "Wow, man, I can't imagine you changing diapers. I've gotta see this!"

"Yeah, well, it's gonna be a trip, all right, but here's the thing. I haven't even been able to talk to Rae." He shook his head. "She hasn't told either her parents or mine because she's waiting for me. I just tried to private message her on Facebook, and her friend responded. She has Rae's phone, and she said Rae's in the hospital. She's got an infection and high blood pressure and stuff. She passed out, and they took her there in an ambulance. And she's living with some woman or something and this friend. She said the baby is okay and they're keeping her for observation." Skylar was just rambling at this point, throwing information at the guys as fast as he could, as if he was in a game of beat the clock.

"Slow down there, bud!" said Nate. "Listen—I mean, she's gonna be okay, right?"

"Well, yeah, I guess so. It's hard to tell when you're private messaging with someone you don't even know. I mean, her friend said she's going to be okay. I swear, guys; I don't even know what to think anymore. For two weeks now all I can think about is how this baby is going to change the course of my life. Then when I thought the flight was going down, I was feeling so guilty to leave Rae to raise the baby all by herself. Then on the flight from Hong Kong, I was back to my selfish thinking and how this baby is going to change 'my' life and how this affects 'me.' I was looking at this baby as God's way of punishing us for sinning.

"But He soon straightened me out and reminded me that this baby is a miracle—I mean, like a real blessing in my life. I'm so determined to marry Rae as soon as I can, tell our parents, and get this all figured out. Now I find out that she's in the hospital. For the first time since I found out … well, I guess I'm just feeling scared now. More than anything I'm just scared." Skylar looked at his two friends with bewilderment in his eyes.

"Scared Rae's not gonna be okay?" asked James.

"Well, yeah, that, and just scared of all the unknowns. How are we gonna pay for a hospital bill? If I'm freaked out with her being in the hospital right now, how am I gonna handle her giving birth, or when the baby gets sick or hurt? I mean, I've always dreamed of being a dad someday, but never did I dream of being one now. I don't even know where to begin!" Skylar's eyes were wide with fear, and he stared blankly at his friends. "What in the world are we going to do?" He looked at his friends as if he was hoping they had all the answers.

James sat back in his chair. "Hmm, I don't know, Sky, but I guess all you can do is just take one day at a time. I mean, I can understand how crazy this all seems and how things are going to change, but my sister had a baby, unplanned, a few years ago. Man, my parents were angry at her for gettin' pregnant, but I can't imagine life without the little guy. I can't wait to tussle with him and play on his toy car track when I get back. My sister just took it all in stride. It's what life threw at her, and she just seized it and ran with it. She could have had an abortion like some do, but of course, she doesn't believe in that.

"So she is raising the little guy on her own; he's totally changed her life. For the better, I mean. He's changed all of our lives. Has it been tough? Oh, you bet! She and my dad go around and round about finances all the time, but she's trying her best to make it all work out. It's not the ideal situation, but he's a happy-go-lucky little guy, and now I can't imagine what life would be like without him."

Nate chimed in, "You know, Sky, that's how it's gonna be for you before you know it. You and Rae have been together forever; you'll get it all figured out. I know your folks; they'll help you guys out."

"Yeah, I know the baby will be a great blessing in my life. I'm just so messed up about all the details and how we're going to make this all work." Skylar sat back in his chair now, threw his head back, and took a deep breath.

"Dude, it's 'cause you're trying to figure it all out on your own. You haven't even talked to Rae yet. Who knows what's she's thinking about everything? I feel like you do need to get to Indiana though. I mean, you weren't planning to see her for a week or two, right?" Nate grabbed his bag noting that their flight was boarding.

Hoisting their duffel bags and slinging them over their shoulders, the three friends walked to the gate. Skylar kept talking. It felt good to talk about it. He needed their help in processing everything. He was relieved to see that their seats were together on the plane. Skylar Weaver had a few ounces of hope that with his friends' help over the next twenty-plus hours, he might get a few things figured out in his mixed-up life.

CHAPTER
Twenty Four

"Oh, hi, Mrs. B," Rae said in a sleepy voice, stretching a little in her bed to find a more comfortable position without disturbing all the monitors attached to her body. "It's so sweet of you to come back and stay with me; you are a true angel in my life!"

"Oh, Rae, it's my pleasure!" Ayala said as she stroked Rae's thick curls. "I brought a few things from home for you—your toothbrush, your bathrobe, a hairbrush, and a few other things I thought you might need. And most important, I brought your phone. We were able to charge it while I was getting your things around. And I have good news," she continued. "Mandy chatted with Skylar on Facebook a little. She told him about your situation. You can read the conversation on your phone," she said as she handed it to her.

"What? Oh, I can't believe I missed him again. This is crazy! Oh well, I'm glad she told him, so he didn't worry when I didn't answer." She grazed her finger over the phone to find the app she needed and began to read the dialogue between Skylar and Mandy.

Her eyes lingered on the last line: "… and tell her I love her." Those words were the best medicine Rae could think of right now. "Wow, it's going to be a while yet till I hear from him. Hopefully, I'll be out of here by then," she said with a yawn.

"I hope so too, but you are here to rest, and that's what you need to do," Ayala said as she fussed over Rae, tucking in her blanket and fluffing her pillow. "I'll just be over in the recliner." She grinned when she saw the worry on Rae's face. "Believe me, I've slept in one of these hospital recliners many times!"

"Okay, I think I can rest knowing Sky is on his way. I'll send him a message and then go to sleep, I promise."

"Sounds like a good plan, Rae."

Rae went back to her phone and brought up the exchange between Mandy and Skylar again. There was so much she wanted to say to Skylar, and yet she had no idea what to write.

"Sky, I'm sorry I couldn't chat with you. I'm in the hospital overnight; hopefully no longer. Baby is fine. I just haven't taken very good care of myself in the last couple of weeks, and my body is taking notice, I guess. I'm so glad you're on your way home. I cannot wait to hear from you and to see you. I miss you so much. I'm sorry you have to come home to these circumstances. I hope this news hasn't ruined the rest of your trip. We will get things figured out together, I know. This little trip to the hospital has really made me anxious to do that! I'll keep my phone with me at all times, so call as soon as you can. I love you! Rae"

She laid her phone beside her and closed her eyes, relieved that her knight in shining armor would soon come and save her. A peaceful rest was right around the corner, she hoped.

Ayala could see the look of peace on Rae's face as she settled into her pillow and slept. Ayala would breathe a sigh of relief when Rae and Skylar told their families about the baby and set their future into motion. She was thankful for Rae and Mandy and the joy they had brought to her life. She worried about them as if they were her daughters. Over the last few months, Ayala felt as if she had indeed experienced what it was like to have a daughter while caring for these girls and it was a good feeling. She had always longed to be a momma, and the time spent with the girls had given her a glimpse of motherhood, even if it was mothering two girls who were about to be mothers themselves.

Ayala slid her recliner back and closed her eyes and wondered how lonely life would be when the girls left after their babies were born. She didn't even want to think about it. She wasn't much up to dealing with loss again when she was still so raw from the loss of her beloved Tim. And sleeping in this recliner, in this place, dredged up memories of those last days she'd spent by his side. No, she thought, as she shook off the feeling. She couldn't think about the loss; she had to live in the moment, taking in each day and enjoying these precious girls as much as she could.

On the other side of town, Mandy Lewis lay wide awake in her cozy bed at Mrs. B's home. The events of the day played in her mind. The fun she had in the garden with Mrs. B, Rae fainting, worrying about her friend, accidentally finding out her mother had died, and an online chat with Rae's boyfriend whom she had been waiting to talk to for months. There was much to think about in many ways. Feeling Rae was safe for now, she found her sleep disturbed by thoughts of her mother.

She didn't even like referring to Patrice Lewis as her mother. Over the last months, however, with everything she had been through, she was sympathetic to what her mother must have gone through to have her. She was thankful her mother had given life to her instead of choosing abortion as she so easily could have. Mandy wished that she knew more about her mother's past, what she was like as a child, who her parents were, how she ended up on the streets— the same streets where she had finally died.

Her mother was a mystery to her. Many times, in her life, Mandy had felt disappointed by this mysterious woman. As a child she desired to be loved by her, and yet she had also hated her. In the last few months, while learning about the gift of God's grace, Mandy wished to give and receive forgiveness from her mother. Now the hope of securing her mother's forgiveness was gone. As Mandy drifted off to sleep, she prayed that God would forgive her for the hate and bitterness she had felt toward her for so long. She drifted into a fitful sleep, where she found herself in her dreamland forest once again.

She was nearing a thicket in the woods. Confused and having lost her sense of direction she was aimlessly wandering through the mass of trees. The night was closing in, and Mandy was frightened. A rustling in the thicket startled her, and she didn't want to go near it for fear it was an animal that would jump out at her. Instinctively she tried to turn and run, but she felt a strong pull to continue past the thicket. She mustered up the courage to walk past the rustling ahead of her. Her heart pounding with each step, she felt compelled to look down into the brush where she heard the rustling.

And there they were, the familiar, unmistakable white spots she had seen before. A fawn! A fawn tangled in the brush. Could it be the same fawn she had rescued from the pit? She drew closer to him to find that he had managed to get his foot tangled up in the undergrowth and was stuck, again! As she peered into his face, she could see by the white spot on the end of his nose that he was the same fawn she had already rescued once. "Well, here you are again. You sure get yourself into some crazy situations, don't you?" she said to the fawn as she worked to free him from the entanglement.

"Now where is your momma?" she asked as she finally freed his foot. The fawn jumped up quickly and scampered down the path. Mandy called after him, "Don't you go gettin' into trouble again!"

The little fawn did not have a good track record in Mandy's opinion, and she was worried he would find trouble again without the guidance of his mother. She scanned the area, hoping to see the big doe standing guard somewhere, but saw nothing but darkness and branches. She had a connection with the little guy by now and felt responsible for him. She thought she should follow him and see that he was reunited with his momma. So she began to pursue this spindly-legged little fellow through the forest. Getting even more lost than she already was, Mandy didn't care. Her concern for him increased with each step. She needed to make sure the little fawn found his mother. She could see that this was also the fawn's mission. He twisted and turned throughout the forest, nose to the ground, trying to pick up his momma's scent. He frantically sniffed and searched while Mandy followed closely behind him.

Mandy began to wonder if the momma was missing or had become a hunter's prize. She shuddered at the thought. At last the little fawn, exhausted from his search, lay down on the dirt path of the forest floor. He was panting, and she could see his heart beating in his tiny chest. His gaunt features showed his weariness and lack of nourishment. Mandy went to him. She nestled down next to him and stroked his soft fur. She understood his grief and despair. Mandy knew what it was like to miss your mother.

CHAPTER
Twenty Five

The ding of the airplane intercom woke Skylar from his deep sleep. He was a little jumpier on this flight than usual, and after his experience flying out of the hill country, he probably always would be. In fact, he had decided it would be a long time until he ever flew again. He had no idea where he was, but he checked his watch to see how close they were to Minneapolis. Only an hour away! Assuming the pilot would deliver the news of their descent, Skylar relaxed in his seat again.

The pilot quickly doused those hopes when he informed the passengers that the tower had rerouted them to Chicago because of thick fog in Minneapolis. There were moans and groans of disappointment throughout the cabin, Skylar's among them. He felt like he was caught in a long dream, hurdling one obstacle after another to reach his destination.

The pilot instructed the passengers to check in at the desk after they went through customs where attendants would help them figure out flights to Minneapolis over the next several hours. He couldn't believe this was happening but had decided he would take advantage of the downtime to finally talk to Rae.

Nate and James had awakened too. "Dude, this is good luck for you," James said excitedly.

"How ya figure?" Skylar sounded confused.

"Man, in Chicago you're a lot closer to Indianapolis than you are to Minneapolis!" James said matter-of-factly.

"So you're suggesting I catch a flight to Indy? I mean, you think that's okay if I don't report back to the program director first thing?"

"Skylar, we've got the weekend off anyway. We don't have to report back until Monday. It might be a whirlwind trip, but I'm guessing it will be worth it to get some things figured out and to make sure Rae is okay. And if you decide to stay longer, well, I'm sure they will understand." James seemed to have it all figured out, and Skylar, for once in his very ordered life, was easily persuaded.

Always one to follow the rules, Skylar sat back as the plane began its descent and let this idea soak in. As he contemplated going home via Indianapolis, a few days late, he allowed worry to creep in again with all the loose ends he would leave dangling.

"So what's it gonna be, Papa?" Nate teased. "You gonna catch a flight to the little woman or what?"

"Wow, I don't know! I mean, I want to but what about the debriefing at the university? I think my parents were talking about driving down on Sunday and all this stuff that has to happen when I get back." Skylar looked at his friends with that wild look in his eye once again.

"Sky, buddy, I know venturing off the path isn't your style, but hey, veering off the 'straight and narrow' got you in this predicament in the first place, bro! Live a little; step out of the boundaries a time or two. You'll survive!" Nate used his "cool" voice, trying to convince Skylar it was okay to have a change of plans.

"Yeah, it's a good idea. It sure would put my mind at ease to make sure Rae's okay, come up with a plan about telling our folks—and it will just help me get a little better grip on things. I've got a credit card I can use for the flights if they're not too much. Or I guess I could rent a car."

"Just get your return ticket back to Minneapolis for Sunday, if you can," James suggested.

"Hey, that's a perfect idea!" Feeling confident now, Skylar grinned. "I like it!" The hour was late, and he was tired. It would be around 4 p.m. Indiana time when he landed. He was guessing that Indy was about a three-hour drive, a little less for the suburb where her college was located. If he could get to the car rental office quickly, he had a good chance of seeing Rae tonight. The thought of seeing her and holding her in his arms made his heart race. This plane could not land soon enough.

Once they were through with the customs check, Skylar said goodbye to his buddies and headed toward the rental car company. He decided to take advantage of the long walk to the rental company and phone his parents. He knew they'd be disappointed but was sure they'd understand.

It was great to hear his dad's voice. Skylar sensed the disappointment in his response after he said he was driving to Indy for the weekend, but he affirmed Skylar in his decision, knowing it had been a long time since he had seen Rae.

"We'll catch you when you get back," his dad said. "Send me a text and let me know you've arrived at Rae's safely," he added.

"Oh, don't worry, Dad. Safety means everything after all I've been through the last couple of days!" Skylar took advantage of the long walk to tell his dad a few details about the almost downed first flight. They ended the conversation shortly before he found the rental car company. "Give Mom a big hug for me," he said before hanging up.

He was able to get an economy car at a reasonable rate. He threw his pack in the backseat, set his GPS, and headed for the highway. He wondered what Rae would think of his appearance. Having lived off the grid for some time and unable to access modern conveniences, he'd let his hair grow quite long, and he now had a pretty decent beard, a first for him. He had hoped to shave and get a haircut as soon as he got home, but Rae would just have to see him with his Grizzly Adams look.

Now for the moment he had been waiting for so long. Once he was out of the city and on the open road, he set his cruise control and dialed Rae's number. He couldn't wait to hear her voice. It had been such a long time.

"Skylar! HI!" The excitement in Rae's voice was music to Skylar's ears.

"Rae, honey, I cannot believe I am finally talking to you!" He had already decided he was going to surprise her and not tell her he was coming. "How are you? Your friend said you were in the hospital."

"Oh, Skylar, I wish I could tell you I'm not here anymore, but I still am." Her tone grew discouraged. "They're keeping me one more night. The woman I've been living with has been here with me, but I told her I'd be okay tonight and sent her home." She was speaking fast and excitedly. "I was so hoping I'd hear from you soon!"

"What in the world is going on, Rae? I mean, first I find out you're pregnant, and if that's not shocking enough, now I find out you're in the hospital! Will you be in for a while? Is the baby okay?" The words *Is the baby okay?* felt so foreign on his lips. He couldn't quit talking long enough to let her answer. "Aw, Rae, I'm so worried about you!"

"Babe, I hate that you have to come home to such a mess. I was hoping you'd pick me up in a week, and then we'd go north and tell our folks about the baby. Of course, all this was supposed to happen after I aced all my classes … but of course, nothing is going as I had hoped.

"It turns out my blood pressure is still high. It hasn't gotten higher since I've been here, which is good, but it hasn't gone down much either. Right now, they say I have gestational hypertension, but it could lead to preeclampsia. I'm so worried because that's a serious condition. The only way to cure it is for me to deliver, and it's way too early. The baby is not due until August."

"Rae, this sounds serious! So what are they saying? —I mean, are they giving you medication?"

"They are, but there are limits on what they can give me because they don't want to use anything that can harm the baby. I've had to lie on my left side most of the time. I'm on a low sodium diet, resting a lot, and they are keeping an IV in with fluids. Oh, Skylar, it's all just very overwhelming. I'm so glad you're back!"

"Man, there is just so much to think about and process, Rae! Right now, though, our focus must be on getting you better. You have to rest and do what they say and just try to get better. You and our baby are the number one priority right now!"

To hear Skylar say "You and our baby" tugged at Rae's heart. She had no idea how he was feeling about the baby, and with all that was going on with her health, they hadn't even talked about that yet. Before she could continue the conversation, the radiologist came in to take her for an ultrasound.

"Oh no, Skylar; someone is here to take me for an ultrasound to check on the baby. Can I call you back? Where are you?"

Skylar was so disappointed that their conversation had to end but glad that they were coming to take a look at the baby. "It's okay, honey. I'm in Chicago, getting ready to board another flight." He hated to lie, but he wanted to surprise her. "I'll call you when I get to the university, so we can talk. By the way, Rae, what hospital are you in anyway?" he asked.

"I'm in Mercy Hospital. Why?"

"Oh, I was just wondering … in case I can't get you by cell phone, I'll try to call your room."

"Okay, Sky. I'm sorry I have to go."

"Stay calm, babe. Everything's going to be okay, I promise. We will talk in detail soon. I love you so much!"

"I love you, Skylar!"

CHAPTER
Twenty Six

To Rae's relief, the ultrasound went well. The baby checked out okay—still very tiny right now, with slim chances of surviving outside the womb. Rae sent up another prayer of thanksgiving for the baby's health, and while she was at it, asked God to please let this precious little one continue developing on schedule.

The ultrasound took an extra-long time since an accident victim had been rushed back to the ultrasound room just before she arrived. The orderly wheeled her into the lobby, where she waited to have the procedure. The ultrasound took a long time as well, as they were checking the baby's size and getting specific measurements. She didn't mind, as she loved catching a glimpse of this miracle on the screen. Afterward a specialist was called in to read everything and make sure she didn't need further scans.

She was tired of lying and sitting and wished she could get up and move around. Waiting in the radiology department looking at dated magazines didn't make matters better either. On her trip back to her room, she wondered if Skylar had tried to reach her yet. She looked at the clock in the hallway, noting that she had been in the radiology department a little over two and a half hours. There was a good chance that he was in Minneapolis by now.

The orderly wheeled her onto her unit. From the unit entrance, she could see into her room. There appeared to be a man there with long hair and a beard. She was alarmed that there was a stranger in her room at first but figured he must be with the night maintenance crew; they sometimes made rounds in the evening to collect trash and bring fresh towels. As she approached the room, she could see that the man was sitting down in the chair in the corner. She glanced at the door frame to make sure she was looking at the right room. Yes, 235, that was correct. She wasn't sure about going in and hoped someone had just made a mistake and gone to the wrong room by accident.

The orderly pushed her into the room. Hesitantly she looked at the man in the chair only to receive the greatest surprise of her life. She could see now that the bearded man had the unmistakable grin that she could pick out of a crowd. The big, toothy, dimply grin of her heart song, her soul mate, her best friend—*Skylar!* "Skylar, what in the world?" she cried as she leaped out of her chair and straight into his arms.

Skylar received her with open arms and breathed her in. He held her as close as her rounded tummy would let him and began to weep like a baby; sobbing uncontrollably into her long auburn locks. Rae was also overcome and started to cry, shaking with emotion while he held her up.

The orderly had left, and the nurse was there to get Rae hooked up again to her IV and monitors. She could see that this was a special reunion and didn't want to bother them, but she still needed to get Rae settled.

"Rae, just let me know when you're ready to get back in bed and hooked up," she said quietly, as she closed the door behind her.

Skylar released Rae from his embrace, held her face in his

hands, and gently kissed her. "You need to get back to resting, little momma," he said as his hand strayed to her tummy.

She laid her hand on his and looked him in the eye. "We're having a baby, Sky!" Her brimming eyes danced with excitement. "Can you believe it?"

Skylar could see the joy in her eyes. She had been growing this life inside of her for six months. They had bonded. She loved this little one with every bit of her being. Skylar could see it. He'd seen that same look in her eyes when she said goodbye before his trip. He saw that look when her brother, Kurt, lay ill. It was the look Rae reserved for those she loved the most. As he looked into her eyes, her love for this little one became contagious, and for the first time since he learned Rae's news, he felt fiercely protective and in love with the baby also.

She squeezed his hand as it lay warm against her abdomen. "Skylar, I'd like to introduce you to your son! I just found out at the ultrasound that we're having a boy!"

Overwhelmed by the news that he would have a son, Skylar was swept by a fresh wave of emotion. He slowly dropped to one knee, pulled the bamboo bag from his pocket, and emptied its contents into the palm of his hand. And there, dressed in her hospital gown and robe, Rae Carver accepted the ring and the proposal from the man she had loved for as long as she could remember. Even though the proposal was far from anything Rae had imagined during all her years of loving Skylar, it was perfect, and she was at greater peace than she had been since the day she found out she was carrying his child.

After she was back in bed, hooked up to the monitors, with the IV fluids dripping once again into her veins, Skylar got permission to stay in her room for the night. Rae's knight in shining armor had finally arrived. He pulled the recliner up to the bed, and there at the bedside of his bride-to-be, he held her hand, and they caught up on the last five months until they both fell into a restful, peaceful sleep.

CHAPTER
Twenty Seven

Mandy took a seat in her "thinking" spot. She had become well acquainted with this park bench, just down the street from Beth Tudor's office. She loved her visits with Beth. Beth helped her plan and organize her thoughts, but she was always mentally and emotionally drained when she left. This meeting with her was especially exhausting as she shared about her mother's death and the fact that the hope of ever seeing her again no longer existed.

Mandy was faced with a mountain of complicated issues right now. Today was the day she would pick up her mother's only possessions at the homeless shelter where she'd resided after she finished her prison time. A daunting task, to say the least, but the most pressing matter was the urgency to make some concrete decisions about her baby as her due date drew near. Her meeting with Beth today was a hard one, and the seriousness of her situation came crashing in on her.

Mandy had come to the harsh realization that she could not

provide for this child who squirmed and kicked inside of her. Not only was she unable to financially provide for a child, but she also lacked a stable support system and a permanent home. But most of all, as much as she hated to admit it, Mandy Lewis knew, she was not emotionally ready to raise a child. Yes, her life was coming together with the help of many people, but she had a long way to go.

Was it fair to bring a child into this instability? Or was it selfish of her to try to get her life together and not include her daughter in the process? Deep in her heart, she knew that her motives were strictly unselfish, wholeheartedly desiring to give this baby, who she loved with all her heart, the best life she could—even if it was without her. Was that how others would view it? Or would they look on her as a selfish individual? And why did she care? She'd never cared what others thought before.

At the Center for Hope, she had met another young pregnant woman in the lobby a few weeks ago. They chatted as they waited for their appointments. As they talked about their plans, Mandy mentioned that she was considering placing her baby for adoption.

The girl gave Mandy a look of shock and informed her that she could never place her baby for adoption. "I made this mistake; I gotta pay for it," she remarked matter-of-factly to Mandy.

Those were bitter words to Mandy. She didn't say this to the woman for fear of hurting her feelings, but in Mandy's mind, a baby was a blessing and not a punishment. She certainly didn't want to keep her baby out of some belief that it was her punishment for poor choices. She had made a mistake, yes, but she was confident that God did not make mistakes.

Mandy had been raised by a drug addict, which dictated the course of her relationship with her mother. She often wondered what her life would have been like if her mother had not been an addict. But lately, she found herself wondering a lot about how her life might have turned out if her mother had placed her for adoption. As she went through this pregnancy, she gained a new appreciation for her mother, specifically that she had chosen life for her. Considering her mother's instability, she often wondered if keeping her to raise on her own was the best thing her mother could have done for her. Now that she was in a similar situation as her mother had been years ago, she understood some of the hard decisions her mother must have faced. She wished she could talk to her about those choices. She wished more than anything she could have had an honest talk with her mother and asked her if she regretted her decision to keep her.

She spent many sleepless nights considering placing her baby for adoption. The thought of handing her over to strangers she knew little or nothing about and never seeing her again terrified her. The idea of raising her on her own terrified her even more. She went back and forth with these thoughts and feelings. Although she had never fully agreed to place her child, she had agreed to look at some of the portfolios from couples wishing to adopt, who had been working with Beth. "Perhaps these will help me decide one way or the other," she had told Beth.

Over the last couple of months, she looked at several portfolios of wonderful people. The couples and families represented on the pages seemed ideal, and of course, she'd have a chance to meet them in person if she wanted.

As perfect as most of the couples seemed, none of the portfolios spoke to Mandy's heart. Some couples were financially stable with high-paying careers, which would inevitably provide a comfortable life for her little girl. Some had children already, and she liked the idea of her daughter having siblings to love and adore her. Two of the couples stated that the adoptive mom would quit her job and stay home with the baby, which appealed to Mandy since time with her mother was always something she desired. But for some reason, not one of the couples presented to her seemed to leap off the page, giving Mandy the clear-cut direction she longed to have. Something seemed to be missing from all of the couples presented to her, but she couldn't put her finger on what it was exactly. Maybe it was because she wasn't ready to let go. Not yet.

At Beth's suggestion, Mandy took the portfolios home and prayed over them. She wasn't quite sure what to say or ask of God, but she laid them all out on her bed, put her hands on them, and asked Him to give her clear direction. She never told anyone, but secretly, she hoped God would direct her through a dream or something specific, as He had been doing with her forest dream. In the days that followed her decision not to abort, she realized God had given her the dream of rescuing the fawn so that her baby also could be saved. Mandy understood now that the chain of recurring dreams of the doe and the fawn in the forest was God's way of guiding her, and she paid attention to them. He had given her unsurmountable strength and wisdom when she needed it most. She wished He would make His will in this situation crystal clear to her. She was growing impatient.

After taking the portfolios home, she prayed fervently, and Mrs. B joined her in prayer. Days passed, and she shuffled through the collection, weighing the pros and cons of each couple, but still she felt nothing. Earlier, at Beth's office, she had hesitantly pushed the paperwork across the table and told Beth she needed more time.

Now, resting on this park bench, Mandy looked down at her large baby bump and realized that time was something she had little of, but she also knew she could not rush into the most momentous decision she would ever make. She closed her eyes as the summer breeze played gently against the folder in her lap. Another portfolio to peruse, a couple who wanted more than anything in the world to be parents and were not physically able. She shook her head at the irony of it all. Here they were; a good-looking Christian couple with money, stability, a beautiful house with a big yard, and a genuine, honest-to-goodness desire to parent. Here she was; a confused, unwed pregnant girl with no money, no home, and no stable support system who was not ready to parent a child. The choice should be a no-brainer for her. It should be easy to see this couple was the best scenario for her baby, but Mandy's brain and heart could not come to an agreement that easily.

Lost in her thoughts, she was abruptly snapped back to reality at the thud of a plastic ball against her shoulder. Startled, she opened her eyes to see a man running toward her. He was ruggedly handsome with a wide grin that seemed to take up his whole face.

He was holding the hand of a darling little girl who wore pigtails high on her head.

"I'm so sorry, Ma'am. I hope we didn't startle you too bad," he said as he gently took the pink plastic ball, embellished with hearts, from Mandy's outstretched hands.

"Oh no, that's okay; no harm done," she said with a half-smile.

"Well, I feel bad. I mean, you were just sitting here enjoying such a nice quiet afternoon and then Ol' Loopity Loo here"—he tousled the young girl's pigtails—"was just out of control with that incredible kick of hers." His eyes were playful, and Mandy could tell he was teasing the young girl.

The little girl threw her hands on her hips, her eyes wide with expression. "I've told you a bazillion times, Uncle Jay, my name is not Loopity Loo—it's Lucy!" She stamped her foot and raised a finger to him. "And you kicked that ball, and you know it!"

Mandy couldn't help but grin at Lucy's adorable admonishment of her Uncle Jay. She raised her eyebrow and gave a sideways glance at Jay to see how he would respond to Lucy's revelation.

"Okay, I guess you're right, little Loopity … oops, I mean Lucy. I guess I'm guilty as charged." With a shrug and a guilty look, he stuck out his hand to Mandy. "I guess little Miss Lucy put me in my place. Please forgive my horrible soccer skills and my feeble attempt to blame it all on little Miss Honesty here."

Mandy shook the man's outstretched hand and said with a nod, "You're forgiven!"

"Ah, good! I'm Jay, by the way, and this here is … well, I guess you know by now. This here is Lucy."

"It's nice to meet you both. I'm Mandy. Do you come here much?"

"My wife and I pick Lucy up occasionally and come here to play and give her mom a little break. Lucy has a new baby brother at home." He gave the girl a playful grin and placed his hand sideways up to his mouth as if he was going to share a secret with Mandy. "Honestly," he announced rather loudly, "we don't really 'want' to bring Lucy with us, but it's the only way we get to play with her really cool toys!" He rolled his eyes toward the girlish pink, heart-emblazoned ball in his other hand.

"Uncle Jay!" Lucy retorted as she grabbed the ball from him and took off running.

"Hey, you, come back here!" he yelled after her as she sprinted away, giggling as she ran. Jay headed out after her, throwing his hand up in the air towards Mandy. "Nice to meet you, Mandy!"

Mandy was mesmerized by the exchange that had just taken place. She watched as Jay chased after Lucy. He caught up to her, lifted her right off the ground, and began to swing her around. The sound of Lucy's laughter was contagious, and Mandy caught herself snickering out loud. *What a wonderfully fun person he is,* she thought. *That little Lucy is lucky to have someone like that in her family.*

Mandy could not keep her eyes off them. She watched as they played and teased each other. Jay pretended to run slowly and acted as though Lucy was too fast for him. She half ran and half skipped and challenged him to do the same. Pretty soon an attractive woman joined them carrying a picnic basket. Jay hoisted Lucy onto his shoulders, and the three of them headed toward the picnic tables nestled under the trees near Mandy's bench.

She felt like a kid seeing cartoons for the first time – all she could do was stare and smile at them. They were such an adorable family, even though Lucy was their niece and not their daughter. They laughed and giggled all the way back. Jay held tightly to Lucy's legs but would dip and sway and pretend he was going to drop her. She, of course, was not scared. Mandy could tell that Lucy adored him and trusted him fully. She only responded with more giggles and loud outbursts of "Stop it, Uncle Jay!"

As they neared Mandy's bench, she quickly dropped her eyes to the portfolio in her lap as if she was engrossed in its contents.

Getting closer to her bench, young Lucy called out, "Hi, Mandy!"

Mandy glanced up with a broad smile. "Well, hello there, Loopity Loo!"

Jay's wife stood there looking up at Jay, confused. "Umm, have y'all met?"

"Oh, Ruth, this here is our new friend Mandy," Jay said with a gesture. "We met when you were back at the car. Um, well, let's just say our ball met her first, and then we met her!" Winking, "I guess you could say our ball introduced us to Mandy."

Furrowing her brow, Ruth said, "I'm so sorry if these two interrupted your peaceful time at the park." The pretty woman poked at Jay. "I just can't send these two anywhere and expect them to behave without me!"

"Oh, it's okay, really. I enjoyed getting to know them and watching them play," Mandy was embarrassed that she had been staring at them and hoped they hadn't noticed.

"Well, I promise I will try to keep them under control over here. Feeding them usually keeps them busy for a little bit, anyway."

"No worries, I trust they will be well behaved. Enjoy your lunch!"

"Wanna have lunch with us, Mandy?" Lucy looked down from her perch atop Jay's shoulders, the noon sun highlighting her pigtails.

"Oh, that's really sweet of you, but I have to catch a bus soon. Thank you anyway, Lucy!"

"Are you sure?" Ruth asked as she patted the picnic basket that hung over her arm. "We have plenty."

"I'm sure, but thank you," Mandy answered as she looked up at Ruth.

It was then that their eyes met, and Mandy was taken aback by the familiarity in them. There was something warm and endearing about Ruth's big brown eyes. Mandy had become keenly aware of how places and people and smells made her feel lately. A woman at the Center for Hope told her it was because women typically were super sensory during pregnancy. Mandy wasn't sure about that, but she did know that when she looked into Ruth's eyes, she sensed peace. It was the same feeling she'd had when she entered the Center for Hope, much like the comfort she felt when she was with Mrs. B, and like how she was drawn toward the doe in her dreams. Mandy sensed that Ruth was a kind-hearted person; someone she'd like to have as a friend. Someone to be trusted. Their eyes were locked on each other for a few seconds until Ruth's eyes opened wide with expression.

"Well, we do have cupcakes, if you change your mind!" She slid her hand into the crook of Jay's arm, and they walked over to the picnic table behind Mandy.

Mandy kept her eyes downcast toward the portfolio in her lap. She was only pretending to be looking at it, however, as the playful banter of the threesome behind her was a sweet distraction. The sounds of a family enjoying life together was music to her. How precious it was when they paused to ask a blessing for the food. Lucy was the one that led out in prayer, and of course, Jay gave a hearty amen in a silly voice, which made Lucy giggle again.

Mandy tried hard to concentrate on the portfolio. The couple in the photograph before her sat against a bridge, looking stylish and in love. Their stats were impressive, but all she could think about was how awesome it would be to find a couple like the one sitting behind her. *This couple in the portfolio looks great on paper, but do they play with each other like Jay plays with Lucy? Do they have so much laughter? Are they as outgoing and friendly? Do I see kindness in their eyes?* Questions rushed through her mind like a raging river. *If only I could find a couple like Jay and Ruth, then I would have peace about placing my baby for adoption,* she thought to herself.

She looked at the time on her phone. The bus would be arriving at the stop in front of the park any minute. She closed the portfolio, picked up the other items she had spread out on the bench, and stuffed them into her bag. She glanced at the picnic table one more time to see Lucy's cheeks smeared with jam and Ruth wiping it off with her fingers. These strangers, turned new friends, had warmed her heart. She wished she could stay and be a spy on their little world all day. *What good parents they will make,* she thought. The screeching sound of bus brakes halted her thoughts as she quickened her pace to the bus stop.

"Well, I guess it's time to call it a day, Miss Loo," Jay said to Lucy as he handed Ruth a baggie of carrots to put away in the basket.

"Aw, do we have to?" Lucy whined. "Can't we stay and play some more, Uncle Jay?"

Jay stretched out his hand to Lucy. "Time to go home and see what your baby brother is up to."

"He's probably just fussing; that's all he ever does," Lucy mumbled. Lucy was trying hard to be respectful, but her face fell in disappointment anyway. As they walked past the spot where Mandy had sat, she spied something on the ground near the bench. "Hey, look," she said, pointing under the bench. "Mandy dropped something."

Ruth stooped to pick up the business card that lay on the ground. She read the inscription:

Beth Tudor
Life Coach
Adoption counseling and placement

She didn't take time to note the address and phone number because she knew Beth Tudor's exact location. She handed Jay the card. Their eyes met. They spoke no words. Words weren't necessary. They both understood that what had taken place in the park that day might very well have been … a divine appointment.

CHAPTER
Twenty Eight

A whirlwind of activity had taken place over the last couple of weeks. Mandy had not approached anyone about finding the article about her mother's death until she knew Rae was doing better. And even then, she didn't know how to go about it. Fortunately, before Rae left to go back to Minnesota with Skylar, she sat down with Mandy and Mrs. B and talked about it. Rae had planned to speak to Mandy the night she brought the article home, but the events of the next few days pushed the newspaper article to the back of her mind. Mandy couldn't blame her.

She really missed Rae. She could use the comfort of her good friend over a bowl of their favorite ice cream right now. But she knew Rae was finally on the mend both physically and emotionally. She had Skylar by her side, she and her baby were well, and the grueling task of telling her parents about the pregnancy was behind her. She and Skylar had a long road ahead of them, but she was confident they would be okay. Admittedly, Mandy was jealous of this. She wished she could say the same thing about her situation. The path that lay ahead for Mandy was full of twists and turns; her destination remained unclear. No matter what she decided, it wasn't going to be easy. But for now, at this moment, she would focus on the task in front of her.

Mandy sat on her bed staring at the battered shoebox that held her mother's personal belongings. It was as if her mother's entire life had been compacted into a tiny box. Mrs. B had encouraged her to take time alone to go through the box and was available in the house if she needed her.

If she'd had her way, Mandy would have just left the box at the shelter. She would have left it just the way her mother had left her so many times. But Rae, Mrs. B, and Beth had all encouraged her to bring it home. Beth suggested that it might give her some closure. *"Closure"? Such a final word*, Mandy remembered thinking when Beth used it. Although her mother had seemed dead to her for many years, nothing had ever felt final where she was concerned. And now that a new beginning with her would never happen, perhaps closure was what she needed. Mandy had reluctantly picked up the box but hadn't looked inside until she was in the comfort of her bed, in the safe place she called home, for now.

The old, beaten-up box was indeed symbolic of her mother's life. It was battered and worn, as her mother had been due to her addiction to heroin. Mandy remembered her mother coming home after a weekend of "using"; she had looked many years older. Her eyes were sunken in; she had bruises and red lines on her arms, and her body resembled a skeleton with skin. Mandy never realized her mother was a drug addict until she saw a poster at the welfare office. The poster showed the warning signs of drug addiction. It described her mother to a T, and the person pictured on the poster even resembled her mother. The box's appearance certainly represented the battered, worn exterior of the mother Mandy remembered.

And then there was the size of the box. That all of her mother's worldly possessions could fit into this small box showed just what a small world her mother had created for herself. Sinking all of herself into things that controlled her, she had stripped herself of all dignity and lost everyone who had ever loved her. The interior of the box plainly spoke to the shallow life Patrice Lewis lived.

Mandy ran her hand along the edges of the box. She didn't know why she found it so difficult to open it. What if it stirred an emotion in her that she did not want to surface? She already was weary from all the up-and-down feelings she was having these days. What if it contained things that would hurt Mandy further? All of these things made Mandy hesitant, but she was also curious, and it was curiosity that encouraged her to finally remove the lid and explore the contents inside.

At first glance, there didn't seem to be much inside really. One of the old photographs her mother had kept in a drawer was there. The edges were bent and torn and the color so faded that Mandy could hardly make out the faces in the photograph. The picture was of a family, presumably Patrice's family, mother, father, and siblings, of whom she never spoke.

There were three tiny hospital bracelets, the kind that you might see on a newborn infant's arm. The dates on them corresponded with the birthdates of her and her sisters. Mandy picked them up and read the stats on each of them, memories of her sisters flooding over her. "One day—one day I will find you," she breathed out a promise. She placed them in her palm by date.

Something about the bracelets stirred up mixed emotions inside her. It wasn't just the pain of missing her sisters but a different kind of emotion as well. She had the feeling of hope. Her mother had kept these bracelets all these years. Through all her moves, prison time, back and forth from pimp to pusher, and even signing over her parental rights, she had kept these bracelets. Perhaps Patrice Lewis did care for her three daughters more than Mandy realized. She wondered what her mother must have felt when she looked at the bracelets. Did she feel hope? Remorse? Sorrow? Pride?

She stared at the bracelets for a good long while. These bracelets were important to her mother. They were symbolic of what she had, what could have been, and maybe even what she hoped was yet to be. Mandy clutched them tightly now. Perhaps her mother had shared the same hope as Mandy. Maybe Patrice Lewis also dreamed of being in a real family someday.

She laid the bracelets aside and picked up three smooth stones from the bottom of the box. One of them was shaped like a heart. Mandy picked up the heart-shaped stone and ran her fingers over its cold, flat surface. Doing so jogged her memory, and she recalled the time that her mother and sisters were wading in a stream at a park. She told each of them they could keep a stone. Mandy remembered finding the heart-shaped one and giving it to her mother. Her own heart was warmed to think her mother had kept it all these years.

There were a few more trinkets in the box—an old keychain, some loose pocket change, her social security card, and a birthday card signed, "With love from Hank."

At the bottom of the box was a well-weathered envelope. Mandy peered inside to find a few old photographs of an apparent trip to a zoo with her sisters that she didn't remember. One was of the three sisters in front of the zoo sign. They all wore knee socks with sandals and short shorts. There were other snapshots taken individually of the threesome in front of various animal cages and a funny one of them acting like monkeys in front of the monkey cage. These were apparently good memories for her mother, and Mandy was sorry she couldn't recall the occasion. She was delighted to see the faces of her sisters again and would cherish these photos of a happy time.

She heard a light rap at the door, "Mandy, are you okay in there?" Mrs. B asked softly.

"Yes, I'm fine," she replied, "You can come in."

The door opened a crack. "Are you sure?"

"Yes, of course." She patted the edge of the bed. "Come, sit with me."

Ayala sat down next to her. "So whatcha' finding in this mysterious box?"

"Well, it doesn't seem like much, but these things were important to my mother," Mandy said. "Just some pictures of us, a photo of what I think must be my mother's family. Oh, and our hospital bracelets, from all three of us sisters. I'd like to do something special with them, like put them in a shadow box with some of these pictures, maybe. I'm sure I can pick up something at the thrift store and make a sort of memory box. Mostly, things that brought up good memories, not bad ones like I feared."

"Mandy, I'm so sorry that your mother is gone," Ayala said as she stroked Mandy's shoulder.

"You know, I spent a lot of time these last few years hating her, feeling like she was already dead and sometimes even wishing she was. When I first learned she was gone, I didn't really care. But since I'm pregnant and all and trying to decide if I want to place my baby for adoption … well, I've been thinking about my mother a little different lately."

"Like, you've been comparing your situation to hers lately?"

"Kind of. All the decisions I have to make—well, I'm guessing she also faced a lot of the same choices as me. I mean, she did choose life for me. I sometimes wonder how my life would be different if she had placed me for adoption, though. I'm pretty sure it would have been better, at least for me. And maybe for her. Some of these things in this box tell me that she did desire to be a good mom. She held on to all that she had of us girls. Maybe the addiction had such a grip on her that she just really needed help, and no one was there or knew how to help her. I think of all the things that could have been in our lives, and it just makes me feel bad for her … for us. I'm not as angry at her anymore; that's getting better for me with time. More than anything, I feel sad that she wasted her life."

"It is sad, Mandy. Your mother missed out on seeing you blossom into a wonderful young woman."

"Oh, Mrs. B, honestly, I don't feel much like a wonderful young woman right now. I mean, if I were such a wonderful woman, I wouldn't be in this situation. I wouldn't be pregnant, first of all. Or at least I would be able to keep my baby and provide a great life for her. Some days it's easy for me to see why my mother may have turned to drugs. Sometimes life just sucks. I mean, I definitely don't want to live my life like she did. I do want to have a better life. I do want to give my daughter a better life than my mom gave me, but I can understand now why she may have made some of the choices she did."

"Well, Mandy, I'm proud of you! I think you are wonderful! I think you're wonderful because you realize all of this. You're setting goals and bettering yourself. You're planning for your daughter. You're planning for yourself. When life punches us in the gut, we can choose one of two things. We can fall to the ground writhing in pain and give up, or we can fight back! Mandy, you've proven to be a real fighter, and I'm proud of you for fighting back. You haven't given up on yourself. You haven't given up on having the life you've always dreamed of having. You haven't given up on the life that you deserve! You haven't given up on giving your daughter the life she deserves, and I think that's pretty amazing," Ayala puffed out her chest with pride for emphasis.

"You know I would be curled up in a heap and completely out of the fight if it weren't for you cheering me on from ringside, Mrs. B! It's been your compassion and the way you have taken care of me these last few months that are helping me see things more clearly. I would never have seen things as I do now if it weren't for you. It's like you have been more of a mom to me in the last few months I've known you then my mother ever was. And believe me, I have definitely needed the wisdom of a mother! You've single-handedly done more for me than I can ever remember my mother doing. I'm realizing though, that my mother simply was not capable of it, because of her addiction. Her addiction was cancer to her—to all of us. I can't thank you enough for everything you've done for me." A tear danced on her lashes. The old Mandy could never have expressed such deep feelings to anyone, but letting Mrs. B know how much she appreciated her seemed natural now, considering her circumstances.

Ayala grinned. "You don't have to thank me, Mandy. I should be thanking you."

"Why in the world would you thank me? I've imposed on you so much!"

"I've been doing a lot of thinking lately. I feel like our meeting on the steps of the abortion clinic was meant to be, for me, as much as it was for you and your baby. I feel like the Lord sent us to each other. You say that you can't thank me enough. Well, the truth is, Mandy, I can't thank you enough! Caring for you and Rae and having your company here in this quiet, lonely house these last months have brought spring back to my long, dark winter. I guess what I'm trying to say is, Mandy, I've always wanted a daughter and never had one. And you, you've longed for a mother for many years. Now, all hope of having your mother again is gone. So I was thinking—"

She paused to pull a folded envelope from her jeans pocket and hand it to Mandy, who opened the envelope and looked at the paper folded inside. "But I don't get it. An application for a name change? What does this mean?" She gave Mrs. B a puzzled look.

"You're twenty-one years old. I can't legally adopt you, but I sure wish I could. I'd love to officially make you my daughter—that is, if you want to be my daughter. The only way to do that is to have you take my last name. If you want to change it, that is. You don't have to change it, but I thought that maybe you could look at it as a fresh start." She slipped her arm around Mandy's shoulders, "What do you think, Mandy? Would you like to be my daughter?"

Mandy looked at the woman before her with shock and joy all rolled into one. These last months in Ayala Banks's home had been the happiest, most contented days of her life. The witness Ayala was to her, the role model she had become, and the love she had lavished on her made Mandy desire to be like Mrs. B more than anyone in the world. At night Mandy would pray, "God, please help me be half the woman that Ayala Banks is." Little did she know it was already His plan. He would answer by giving her a real family with this beautiful woman, Ayala Banks!

"Yes, yes—thank you, Mrs. B! I do want to be Mandy Banks. It would be a great honor to be your daughter!" She could only cry. She cried tears of happiness, and they spilled freely all over her and her new mother, who embraced her in a big warm motherly hug.

"I would love to have a fresh new start, a chance to put Mandy Lewis behind me and start over."

"Well, don't go too far there, little missy! I don't want you to forget about Mandy Lewis. God has been using all these struggles in your past to mold you and shape you into the woman He desires you to be. All those things in your past are being used to strengthen your character. You're just changing your name to seal our commitment to each other as mother and daughter. You are charging forward into a bright future ahead and not living in the past." Ayala gave her new daughter another squeeze.

They sat on the bed and chatted as a mother and daughter would do for some time. They talked about the future. They set goals of taking vacations together and having mother-daughter shopping trips. They spoke of being a family, an unconventional one, but a family, which Mandy had longed for all the same. Mrs. B suggested Mandy get dressed and they would go out for a celebratory dinner and then, of course, ice cream!

As Mrs. B left the room, Mandy gathered up the contents of her mother's box. As she stacked the zoo photos up and began to place them in the envelope, something caught her eye in the top picture. It was a picture of her sitting cross-legged in front of an animal pen. Her hands were gripping the wire of the enclosure as she peered down at an animal lying on the ground close to the fence. Mandy brought the picture up close to her to see more clearly the telltale white spots of a fawn, with the legs of his mother in the photo as well. The doe was bent over him, her nose nuzzling his neck. Mandy wiped a tear from her eye, remembering the lost fawn from her most recent dream. She said out loud, "Looks like we've both found our mother."

CHAPTER
Twenty Nine

"Carver men looking good, huh, Dad?" Kurt asked as his dad straightened his son's tie.

"Yep, we handsome dawgs!" Rick Carver replied in his best Southern drawl.

"Sky's finally gonna be my brother!"

"Yes, after today you will finally get Skylar Weaver as your brother, Kurt. Well, technically your brother-in-law, but you can call him brother if you want. I'm sure Sky is okay with that." Rick gave his son's tie one last tug. "Why don't you go find Mom now, son."

Rick Carver wished he shared Kurt's excitement about his sister's wedding day. Rick had often envisioned walking his beautiful Rae down the aisle. Those visions always involved the same man she would marry today, but never had they included walking her down the aisle under these circumstances. Never in a million years could he imagine that he would give his daughter away to Skylar Weaver ... six months pregnant!

Rick now fiddled with his own tie. His reflection in the mirror showed the strain of the last three weeks. Neither he nor Nancy had slept much since the video call they received, from an Indiana hospital room, three weeks ago that rocked their world and brought all their hopes and dreams for their daughter to a screeching halt. That call when Skylar and Rae broke the news to them: that they were engaged, that they were pregnant, and last but certainly not least, that Rae was in a health crisis. Since that moment, Rick and Nancy Carver, as well as their daughter's soon to be in-laws, John and Cindy Weaver, had all experienced every emotion possible. Or at least, so it seemed.

First came shock and disappointment. Of course, the Carvers and the Weavers were disappointed that Rae and Sky had broken their purity commitment to each other, even if it was just one time, and they had sought forgiveness over it. Mostly, they were disappointed that their goals and dreams and everything they both had worked so hard for were being interrupted and changed. Rick especially had such big hopes and dreams for Rae to graduate from his alma mater and eventually work alongside him in his pharmacy. She managed to get through the last week of finals after her hospital stay, but barely. And now she was filling out the paperwork to transfer everything to Minnesota to finish close to home and without scholarship assistance. Grateful that Rae planned to finish her schooling, Rick and Nancy were willing to make whatever sacrifices they needed to ensure this happened. Offering their basement to the newlyweds as their first home and taking the extra financial responsibilities of making up for her scholarship money was just the beginning.

Probably the toughest emotional struggle was that of shame and disgrace. Rae and Skylar were exemplary role models in their church and community, well known to be godly, respectable, and level-headed. And now, his beautiful little princess was the "girl who had to get married." It was tough for him and Nancy to face their peers. Even though they had felt loved and supported by those closest to them, no doubt gossip and horrible things were being said about his sweet, sensitive Rae. A deacon in his church, some days Rick found it hard to stand up under the humiliation of it all.

What if Rae did go on to take over the pharmacy for him someday? Would this situation be the one thing that defined her in the eyes of the community? Would she always have to battle the shame of a premarital pregnancy? Rick tried not to care what others thought, but being a businessman in a tight-knit, conservative community, and a deacon in their church, he feared that his whole family would be under a microscope of scrutiny from now on.

The fact that neither set of parents knew any of this was going on until six months into the pregnancy was especially hard to grasp. They just felt like bad parents. Nancy had shared with Rick that she felt as if she didn't know her daughter anymore. Neither of them could shake the feeling of disconnection with their daughter. Both he and Nancy had always had such a close relationship with Rae. In the past, Rick felt as if he and Rae could talk comfortably about anything. But now, he just felt deceived. So much deception over the last few months from someone he thought he knew so well had made him shake his head in disbelief many times over the previous few weeks.

Rick was finally coming around to understand why Rae waited to tell them. He supposed that if he and Nancy had found themselves in their shoes at that age, they most likely would have done the same thing, but it stung all the same. Rae had always been truthful and honest with them growing up. All these secrets and lies along the way just plain hurt, there was no getting around that. He couldn't help but think that if they had known earlier, it would have made things easier for all of them in the long run. So many "what ifs" went through Rick's mind.

But as Rae reminded them when they brought this up, she would not have had the opportunity to meet the beautiful woman, Ayala Banks, who had been such a great help to her. She also would not have had the privilege to be a witness to her new friend Mandy. Rae couldn't quit talking about these two women who had impacted her so much. Rick was forever grateful to Mrs. Banks for all she had done for Rae. He also recognized that his daughter had learned to completely rely on God in her life, which was a blessing during this unsettling time.

And then there was the chaos that ensued once Skylar brought her home a couple of weeks ago. Scrambling to find them both summer jobs, getting Rae connected with doctors, and readying the basement for newlyweds and a baby was overwhelming. Then there were meetings with their pastor, obtaining a marriage license and just trying to adjust to the fact that his daughter, his little girl, with the sweet bouncy red curls, was … pregnant.

It was a lot to take in, and Rick and Nancy had cried many tears over the last few weeks. They sat with Skylar's parents, alongside Skylar and Rae, when they met together to try to come up with a plan and cried with them as well. Tears for shattered dreams as well as tears of thanksgiving. They cried tears of gratitude over God's provision for Rae when she became ill and for Skylar in his near plane crash. There were also tears of joy for the precious life that would soon become their grandchild. Some days they all just felt like a "hot mess," which was the term Rae used to describe it. And yet, with Rae's fragile condition and blood pressure issues, they had to rein in their emotions much of the time so as not to upset her.

The last several days had been one big emotional roller coaster ride for all of them. Simply put, this turn of events in their lives was hard. Rick and Nancy knew that the next couple of years would be a challenge for all of them, but they loved Rae completely. And even though Rick had experienced full-on discouragement and anger with Rae at times lately, his heart was wholly devoted to her and her new adventure of being a wife and mother. None of this was how he had foreseen Rae and Skylar's future together, but he would stand beside them no matter what; because that's what daddies do. Rick Carver would never give up on his daughter—or his first grandchild!

After all, Skylar Weaver was a godly man. He couldn't imagine Rae with anyone else. Rick admired Skylar and Rae for seeking God in these decisions. It was humbling to Rick that Skylar wanted to make Rae his wife, as soon as possible. Rick was the first to admit that Skylar was human, and all humans make mistakes. Sky and Rick had talked man to man, and he had asked for Rick's forgiveness. Skylar had proved himself to be a man of integrity, and Rick was happy to give him his daughter's hand in marriage. Rick knew that Skylar's family would stand in support of the newlyweds as well. Their families had raised these kids together and would enjoy grandparenting together.

Rick headed down the stairs at Community Christian Church to find the blushing bride. Rae and Skylar insisted on being married by Reverend Dan. They wanted a simple ceremony where they would say their vows in front of their immediate family and, of course, Rae's best friend, Sadie, who had already married them several times over when they were in preschool.

Rick was okay with this arrangement, but he had his own requirements for her wedding day. Just one thing was on his list: that he could still walk her down the aisle. He found her at the bottom of the stairway, wearing a simple dress that fit snugly around her baby bump. Her long red curls were swept into a loose bun with long wisps hanging randomly. She looked as pretty as he'd ever seen her, and his heart so filled with love for her that he felt like it might burst open.

"Oh Rae, you look stunning, honey!" he said, choking back the tears.

"Daddy, please don't get me started with the crying again," Rae replied. "I want this day to be happy. I know none of this is how I dreamed it would be but I am happy." Her gorgeous green eyes danced as they looked deep into his. "The most important part of all my dreams is still coming true. I'm still marrying the man I adore, surrounded by those I love the most, and best of all, you're walking me down the aisle. I can't imagine anything better!"

Rick extended his arm, flashed a big smile, and said, "Well, let's do this, little lady!"

They giggled up the stairs, and she joked that they both should try waddling up the aisle. As they reached the sanctuary doors, they both sported big smiles. At the altar stood Skylar flanked by his best man, Kurt, and his family, including his sister Sage who lived out east. On the other side were Sadie and Nancy. The pews were empty; only their family would share in this special day. Pastor Dan's wife began to play a beautiful piano piece that Rae had selected. All eyes went to the back of the sanctuary.

Skylar's heart skipped a beat at his first glimpse of his beautiful bride. He couldn't believe the turn of events in his life in just a matter of a few weeks. Only a short time ago he was saying goodbye to the Cambodian villagers that he had grown so fond of, and now today, he would take the hand of his sweet Rae to be his wife. In just a few months he would be a dad! It was all surreal and overwhelming to think about, but he decided he was going to savor the moments in this day. He vowed to himself that he would not allow the worries of the future ahead, or the grief of the experiences he'd left behind in Cambodia, to bog him down, for today he would marry the most beautiful girl in the world.

CHAPTER

Thirty

Climbing the stairs to the entrance of Beth's building was getting more cumbersome for Mandy. She stood on the top step and paused to catch her breath. This visit could very well be one of her last meetings with Beth before her baby's birth. Many things had transpired in the final weeks of her pregnancy.

Beth saw Mandy standing on the porch and came out to greet her. "Mandy are you okay?"

"Yes, it's just that waddling is not all that it's cracked up to be," she responded with a laugh.

"Well, waddle on in here and have a glass of lemonade," Beth said, holding the door for Mandy.

Beth poured two large glasses of lemonade and set them down on the table. She had papers laid out in front of her. With her glasses on her nose, she glanced at them quickly before officially starting their meeting. "Well," she said as she looked up at Mandy with a smile, "did you go get your mother's belongings from the homeless shelter?" Her face grew more serious as she asked.

"Yes, I did go get them," Mandy replied.

"And ...?" Beth pushed for more details.

"Well, I opened the box, and then I found my mother!" Mandy had a smirk on her face.

"What in the world are you talking about, Mandy?" Beth could see she was up to something.

"You see, I was looking through the box, feeling kind of down as I went through her measly belongings. The things in the box wouldn't mean much to anyone else, but they were special to my mother, and so now they are special to me.

"Thanks for suggesting I get it, by the way. You talked about it bringing me closure, and I guess you could say that it did. Like I was telling Mrs. B, I hated my mother for so long. That box gave me a little glimpse of her heart and what a sad, miserable, and lonely person she must have been. I feel like she wasted her life. Mrs. B and I talked about forgiveness and how you can forgive someone without them even asking for it. I like that, and I'm working on that with my mother."

"And so, when you say you found your mother, you mean you found her heart?"

"Oh no, here's the good part. So I'm sitting on the bed looking through this box and feeling sad. I was missing my sisters too, because there were pictures of them and their hospital ID bracelets and lots of memories popping up while I looked through. Then Mrs. B walked in and handed me an envelope with a name change form in it."

"A name change? What for?" Beth asked, surprised.

"Well, since I'm twenty-one, she can't officially adopt me, but I can at least change my name to Banks and then she can officially be my mom!" Mandy beamed with pride. "A new name and a fresh new start!"

"Wow! What exciting news!" Beth got up from her chair and hugged Mandy. "My visits with you are always so full of surprises,

Miss Mandy Banks!" Beth teased. They chatted a bit about the possibilities this fresh new start would open up for Mandy.

Beth looked at the clock on the wall, "Well, Mandy, since our time is limited, I suppose we should get down to business. Your due date is quickly approaching. I know you've taken labor and delivery classes, but as we work on your birth plan, we've never established who will be your labor and delivery coach. That is, if you are planning to have someone there with you."

"Oh, I hope that Mrs. B, I mean my mom, will be my coach! It will be a good experience for her to witness the birth, since she's never had a baby. I will be so much calmer having her there, I'm sure. I haven't officially asked her but plan to. I wanted to run it by you for sure."

"Okay, perfect, great plan!" Beth and Mandy continued to talk about the birth and what her wishes were for anesthesia and birthing methods.

Mandy wanted very badly to have a natural labor and delivery. "I want to feel the pain of having her," she told Beth. "I know that sounds crazy, but my life has had much pain. These last few months I've learned that the greatest things in life involve sacrifice and hard work—and sometimes pain. Like my friend from the factory used to say, 'No pain, no gain.' This baby girl is the greatest thing to ever happen to me; I want to experience the pain and the hard work of bringing her into the world. Because of her, I've already gained so much." Mandy looked at Beth with confidence in her decision.

"Well, so be it, Mandy. I can respect that for sure, but just remember, there is no shame in getting something for pain if you need it, okay?"

Mandy agreed. She had been taking classes at the Center for Hope and felt as prepared as she could be for the actual labor and delivery. It was the days following the birth that worried Mandy. She confided in Beth about these issues, and they spent a good deal of time talking about how she would feel both mentally, emotionally, and physically. Beth assured her that she would have lots of support in Mrs. Banks's home, and she could visit her for extra comfort and encouragement if need be.

Beth talked to her about government programs and assistance Mandy could use until she was able to go back to work. Mandy knew she would have to get a better job than her current thrift store position, so she and Beth chatted about possibilities in that area as well.

"I love Mrs. B, and I'm so grateful to be her daughter now, but I am also an adult, and I know that after I recover from giving birth, I will need to find a place to live. Mrs. B and I have talked about that and the importance of me keeping up with my independence and finding my way with her support and guidance," Mandy continued. "I'm ready for that also; I'm ready to take on real life. Even though it's a little bit scary."

"Well, the Mandy I know is strong and courageous and not afraid to move forward. You'll be on your feet and find your way in no time," Beth replied. "Remember, He has plans to prosper you and not harm you, plans for a hope and a future, Mandy. You're on your way!"

"Oh Beth, you've helped me so much! Thank you," she added, trying hard not to cry again. Beth assured her that she would miss her once her baby was born and she no longer needed her services but did encourage her to continue getting counseling from her if she needed to.

Beth looked at her watch and informed Mandy that she had another appointment she needed to make. Mandy scooted her chair back and bent over to pick up her purse. As she straightened, she felt a pop low in her abdomen, and before she knew it, she was sitting in a puddle of water.

"Umm, Beth, I think my water just broke!"

Beth turned quickly toward Mandy. She could see water dripping from the chair and onto the carpet. "Oh, no, Mandy, I would say your water definitely broke!" Beth muttered and turned this way and that, in evident confusion. "Just stay seated, Mandy. I'll call Mrs. Banks and have her meet you at the hospital."

Although she was a bit shaken, Mandy remained calm—calmer

than Beth seemed to be. "It's okay, Beth. I have my phone right here. I'll give Mrs. B a call if you want to get a towel or something, so we can clean up this mess."

"Oh yes, a towel. Yes, that's a good idea," Beth scratched her head as if she had no idea what a towel was. She promptly left the room in pursuit of a towel, or at least Mandy hoped that was where she was going. Mandy calmly picked up her phone and called Mrs. B. She sure hoped she was home; she desperately needed her mother.

CHAPTER
Thirty One

Ayala could smell the fresh paint as she unwrapped the contents of the box and pushed the tissue paper away. She ran her fingers over the surface of the wooden sign that she pulled out and let them brush each letter: "A LIFE RESCUED." The title was perfect. She couldn't wait to hang it above the door to her home. Her home, now turned halfway house, for girls in a crisis pregnancy.

Ayala had promised Tim she would continue to do the good work God had designed for her to do in those days before he died. She had been so blinded by her grief in the months following his death that she was unable to see just exactly what that work was. Lately, God had been making that crystal clear to her, and she knew it was time to step out in obedience to His calling and trust in His leading.

Not only had God graciously given Ayala the daughter she had always longed for by opening her home abruptly to two young girls who were in crisis pregnancy situations; but He had also affirmed where He was calling her in ministry. After much prayer and encouragement from the director at the Center for Hope and her prayer partners, Ayala had decided to open her home as a halfway house for girls such as Mandy and Rae.

She hoped to provide a place of refuge for girls who had chosen life for their baby but had nowhere to turn. When she was petitioning God about this she came across Psalm 91:14 in the New Living Translation: "The LORD says, 'I will rescue those who love me. I will protect those who trust in my name.'" This verse reminded her of how God had rescued her so many years ago and how He had continued to watch over her, especially in the past year.

She wanted to provide a place where girls with unplanned pregnancies could experience rescue and protection from God while in her care. "A Life Rescued" would be the name of her new ministry. The title reflected her own life as well as the hope for the ministry. She desired that everyone who walked through her door would experience rescue in some way.

Today began the first step in seeing this ministry come to life, as she made it official with her new sign. She had already been doing a practice run with Rae and Mandy, and they were compliant little guinea pigs for her! She had teased them about this as she bounced these thoughts and ideas off them in the last couple of months.

She laid the sign to the side and dug through the box to find the brackets to hang it. They were hidden deep in the wrappings. She gathered the box and had begun to tear it apart for the recycling bin when her phone on the counter rang.

As she got closer to the phone, she could see Mandy's name on the screen. Ayala kept her phone close by her these days as Mandy was due to deliver her baby any day, and now with the name popping up on the screen her heart skipped a beat at the thought that this might be "the call."

"Hi, Mandy! What's up?" Ayala chirped after sliding the toggle switch to answer.

"Mrs. B, my water just broke at Beth's office. Any chance you can get me?

Ayala's heart began to race. "Of course, I'll come get you! I'll grab your bag and be right there. You just sit tight, and I'll be there in a jiff!" Her voice had risen an octave.

"Okay. And Mrs. B?" Mandy paused, making sure she was still on the line.

"Yes, Mandy?"

"Umm, I've never asked this before, and if you don't want to that is fine, but would you be willing to be with me during labor and delivery?"

"Oh Mandy, I wouldn't miss it for the world! I'll be there soon!"

Ayala hurried about, grabbing Mandy's bag and throwing a few things for herself into another bag. "Oh, my camera, I can't forget my camera," she said out loud as she scurried throughout the house. Soon the bags of necessities were tucked neatly into the backseat, and Ayala was on her way.

She must have had a bit of a lead foot on the gas pedal because within an hour after Mandy's phone call she was entering the doors of Mercy Hospital again. There were no conflicting feelings from days past, for today she'd witness here the birth of an extraordinary baby! Ayala was excited to go through the birthing process with Mandy. She was excited, of course, because it was her new daughter's baby, but also because this was a rescued baby. Freed from the grip of abortion; this baby was special. Unlike her own baby, whom she never got to meet this side of heaven, this baby had received the gift of life. This little darling had been rescued from the hands of the abortionist by the gentle nudging of Jesus. It was the day that Jesus pushed Ayala toward a young girl, faint on the steps of the clinic, to step out in boldness and tell her story.

This little girl was special indeed, and Ayala could not wait to meet her. God had a great purpose for this little one, Ayala felt sure of that! She pushed the fourth-floor button on the elevator panel and returned to the maternity floor, where she had left Mandy while she went to park the car.

She found Mandy wearing a hospital gown decked with monitors and wires; nurses bustled around her. Mandy put out her hand when she approached, and Ayala was quick to take it. "Are you having any pain yet?" she asked with concern in her eyes. The swooshing sounds of the baby's heartbeat now filled the room as the monitors did their work.

"No, not really," Mandy said with disappointment.

"Oh, don't sound so disappointed," quipped a nurse with a giggle. "You'll eventually wish you weren't having any pain!" She went on to explain to Mandy and Ayala what all the machines were for, what they measured, and what the graph lines on the screens meant. She gave Ayala a crash course on coaching Mandy with her breathing once the contractions hit. She also informed them that this might be a long evening, as labor could last for hours.

Eventually Mandy's doctor came in to examine her and announced that she was dilated but had a ways to go. He encouraged Ayala to grab a bite to eat and settle in for a long night. She made a quick trip to the cafeteria but wasted no time getting back to Mandy's side.

Once the contractions started, Ayala found that she had her work cut out for her. She wanted to respect Mandy's wishes not to take anything for pain, but she begged her to take the medications anyway. Mandy was firm in her decision, and so Ayala became creative in ways to calm her and get her through each contraction.

She fed her ice chips between contractions, rubbed her back, quoted scripture, prayed over her, and held her hand. *So this is what it feels like to be a mother,* Ayala thought to herself: *hurting alongside your child and wishing to take her pain.*

She sincerely wished she could take on Mandy's pain and ease her discomfort, even if only for a little while. But she loved and respected her enough to know that she wanted to feel this pain. Mandy was fiercely strong and independent. Ayala knew this was something she needed in this process, and she would not take that from her.

The labor went on for hours. Nurses and aides changed shifts, and they all had varying advice for Mandy on ways to handle the pain, from breathing techniques to standing, walking, sitting on a ball, and rocking back and forth to various ways to lie down. Mandy was willing to try them all, and she found some did bring relief for a short time.

Night rolled into morning, and neither Mandy nor Ayala had slept. At last, an examination showed that Mandy was fully dilated and ready to push. Just as the nurses were setting things up and preparing for the birth, the baby's monitor began to chime. Panic ensued, as the fetal heart rate had dropped significantly. There was concern that the baby might be in real danger.

After a final examination, Dr. Menninger delivered the unwelcome news to Mandy that he would have to do an emergency cesarean section to ensure the baby's safe delivery. Since Mandy had opted not to have an epidural early on, there was no time for one now. They would administer anesthesia that would put her in a deep sleep.

Mandy was scared to death and brokenhearted that she would not get to see her baby be born. She broke down in tears, and Ayala cried alongside her. Ayala held her hand tight until they wheeled her away. "I love you, Mandy," she called out to her.

"I love you too, Mom!"

Ayala stood in the doorway of the empty delivery room, staring down the hallway of the maternity ward with Mandy's words, *I love you too, Mom,* echoing in her ears. The irony overcame her. She had not physically given birth, but today, in this place where the miracle of life happens, she had truly become a mother.

CHAPTER Thirty Two

The little fawn nestled close to Mandy, and she could feel his little heart beating. She had created quite a bond with the little fellow. She was incredibly fond of him and very protective too. The sun was low in the sky, filling the forest with mystical light beams and softness. Mandy knew that finding the fawn's mother was imminent. There was no way she would leave him, though, until she knew he was safe, sound, and cared for in a way that she could not provide. Their rest time was over, and she gave her spotted little friend a gentle push to awaken him. He yawned and stretched and shook his head as if to shake the sleep from his eyes.

He stayed close to Mandy's side. She had become his security; the place where he felt safe. "Come, little one, let's see what we can find," she said, scratching behind his ear. She and the fawn began their adventure once more, traipsing aimlessly through the thickets and brush looking for traces of his mother.

As they walked, Mandy thought about what she would do if

she couldn't find the doe. She was determined not to leave his side. Oddly, Mandy didn't seem to care that she too was lost, in a forest, having no idea where she was. She wasn't afraid. Her focus was on this baby deer and finding safety for him. Once she did, then she would worry about herself. All that mattered now was the well-being of the one left in her care. As crazy as it was, Mandy was wholly committed and deeply devoted to a wild animal baby of the forest. In a sense, this fawn had become part of her, and it wasn't just obligation that was driving her but a real sense of compassion and love for this sweet little life. He was helpless, and Mandy was determined to do whatever was necessary to make sure he was safe and happy.

They searched and listened, and for a moment Mandy felt a wave of panic. *What if I don't find his momma? How will I care for this fawn?* A warm breeze blew the wisps of hair from her face. It was refreshing, and she closed her eyes to take it in. There, in the stillness of the moment, she sensed God's presence. The soft wind blew, and with it came God's gentle truth in Psalm 56:4, embracing her and filling her senses.

"I praise your promises! I trust you and am not afraid. No one can harm me."

An overwhelming sense of peace filled her soul. She made up her mind that they would continue their search and trust in God to work out the details. She breathed a prayer of thankfulness for the promise of His protection. She relied on God to lead them, and with fresh determination, they continued.

They wandered through the forest, over a brook, and to places filled with nothing more than trees. It seemed they had been traveling for days. She felt there must be a clearing or an opening somewhere, but at each turn, the woods engulfed them more deeply. The little fawn grew tired at times and stopped along the way. Thinking he was most likely hungry, she had nothing to sustain him except the comfort of her touch as she encouraged him along. Finally, the fawn could go no longer. Exhausted from the walk and the lack of nutrition, he could not make his tiny legs carry him anymore.

Mandy scooped him into her arms, and they began to walk through the woods, together, as one. The burden of his weight wasn't too cumbersome at first, but the longer they walked, the heavier he seemed.

Eventually becoming weary herself, Mandy stopped and sat down on the cool forest floor. She pulled the fawn close to her and buried her head in his downy fur. She cried out to God. "I want to trust You, God. I know, in my heart, You are with me, but right now I don't feel You. I feel weary and hopeless. The baby fawn is weak, and I have no way of helping him."

She recalled Psalm 82:4, which said, "Rescue the weak and the needy; deliver them from the hand of the wicked."

We are weak and needy. "Please, Father, rescue us!" She groaned in prayer as her strength and resolve were fading. "Please, God, show me the way; I don't know where to turn! I don't think I can do this anymore!" Her desperate pleas were no longer silent, she cried out to God with all her might in the great woods.

Then another scripture reassured her—Psalm 91:14: "The LORD says, 'I will rescue those who love me. I will protect those who trust in my name.'"

Rescue! There was that word again. Her present-day reality now became intertwined with the thoughts of her dream cycle. In the last nine months of her life, Mandy had heard the word *rescue* many times. It was in her recurring nighttime missions of rescuing a fawn. Rescue was the foundation on which Mrs. B was building her mission, and she talked about being rescued when relaying her testimony. Mandy had experienced rescue in many ways: rescued by Mrs. B; rescued by her Savior; she and her baby rescued!

"O God, I need you … please strengthen me!" She cried out with surrender, "Rescue me!"

"O LORD, my strength and my stronghold, my refuge in the day of trouble" came the words from Jeremiah 16:19.

This new promise from God's word comforted Mandy, and she was once again encouraged by the reminder that she was not doing this alone. God was with her. She could grasp tightly to His hand,

and He would lead them. She had to trust. Her energy must come from Him. He was her strength and stronghold, her refuge.

She held the fawn with one arm and wiped the tears from her face with the other. She rose up from the ground, clutching the fawn to her chest, and took a deep breath. She took a moment just to stand and try to get some direction. It was useless; everywhere she looked were trees and more trees. North of her though, there was a glimmer of light that vaguely shone through the branches.

"Well, I guess we will go where there is light, little one," she said with uncertainty. As she walked, she shot up short prayers to God. "You are my stronghold in times of trouble. —Rescue Your weak and needy servants, God. —Show us the way, God." With each step, she breathed out a prayer to God. With each step, she became more sure-footed as she leaned on Him. For the first time in her forest adventure, she and God walked together. She felt complete assurance of His direction and provision. She found renewed strength and energy by calling out to Him, "Strengthen me, God. Bring us help in our time of need, Father. Rescue us!"

As Mandy walked and talked with God, the light grew brighter, and she walked closer to it with expediency in her step. A sunbeam streamed through the trees, and her heart raced. She picked up her pace so that the little fawn bounced lightly in her arms. And then Mandy came to an abrupt halt. Her eyes grew wide as just beyond the trees at the forest's edge was a meadow filled with tall green grass and bright yellow wildflowers. There in the distance, nibbling on the grass, was a small herd of deer. Four does, beautiful and graceful as they ate their fill from the rich abundance of grass.

Mandy did not know if the fawn's mother was among them, but she was confident that the Lord had walked her to this place. She knew in her heart this was where the young fawn belonged because this was where the Lord had led them. She made no sudden moves so as not to startle the herd but gently lowered the little one to the ground and gave him a gentle nudge. He moved ahead but stopped short, looking back at Mandy as if ready to run right back to her. Mandy stayed low and didn't move. She could hear grunts from the grazing does. The fawn's ears perked at the familiar sounds, and he turned toward them.

Mandy took a deep breath and prayed silently. "O Father, You have walked us to this place. Please give the fawn the courage to go where he belongs. And Father, would You please give me the courage to let him go?"

It was as if she could hear God's answer, from Deuteronomy 31:6: "Be strong and courageous. Do not be afraid or terrified, for I, the LORD your God, go with you; I will never leave you or forsake you."

Mandy watched cautiously as the little fawn took a few steps toward the herd. She wished with all her might that she could give him a big push, but she knew he had to go on his own. A few more steps, and then with perked ears and fresh curiosity the little fawn walked as fast as his weary legs would carry him, right to the grazing does. One of the does went to him and began to sniff and lick him; others came over to investigate and do the same. Mandy started to rise, ready to rush in and snatch him up if the does rejected or hurt him. But to her satisfaction, the little fawn seemed to love the attention, and finally, he found one who would provide nourishment for him as well.

Mandy wiped a tear from her eye, overcome with relief and joy for the fawn. The scene before her was surreal, and she soaked it all in. Nature at its finest; a community of does providing for an orphaned fawn. She realized how she missed the weight of him in her arms, the feel of his heartbeat, and the softness of his fur. But he was where he belonged, and the peace she felt in her heart was greater than the ache of those things she missed about him. She had allowed God to lead her, and He took her right where they needed to be, straight where the fawn belonged.

Still hidden in the trees, she gazed at the scene in the meadow. Her long journey was over, and she was content. She was enjoying the serenity of the moment when suddenly things grew hazy. Mandy thought she was just tired and tried unsuccessfully to wipe the sleep from her eyes. The scene went in and out of focus, and she strained to see. She could barely make out the image of the fawn anymore. The gentle sounds of the meadow intermingled with the harsh beeps and voices of her reality. Piercing through the soft sounds of the meadow was the undeniable sound of a baby crying.

"Mandy? Mandy, honey?" The nurse called out to her amid the chaos of the recovery room. "You came through your C-section just fine, Mandy." She felt the dampness of a warm cloth on her face. "Can you hear your baby? Do you want to see your daughter?"

Mandy mumbled something inaudible to herself and the others in the room. Her mouth felt full of cotton. She tried desperately to open her eyes, but her eyelids were too heavy.

"It's okay, Mandy," the nurse assured her. "We'll let you wake up a little. There's no rush. Your daughter will go to the nursery and wait until you're ready to see her!"

"My daughter?" Mandy smiled at the words as she formed them in her mind. "She is here, my baby is here, and I can't even open my eyes to see her." Mandy fretted in her confused, sleepy state.

Her battle to wake up continued as the anesthesia started to wear off, and the aftereffects of it started to kick in. Mandy felt miserable in every way. She didn't know where she was, why she couldn't seem to wake up, or how she had gotten there from the forest.

Even though everything seemed foggy, she did remember someone saying her C-section went well and her baby was fine. She felt incredibly confused and disconnected, and she didn't understand why she couldn't hear the baby crying anymore. She moved her hand down to her abdomen. Although swollen and tender, it was soft and flat; her accustomed baby bump was no longer there.

Her baby's absence from her body left her with an overwhelming ache in her heart. Where was she? Where had they taken her? She began to cry through her misery and mustered up the strength to scream out loud, "I need to see my baby!"

CHAPTER
Thirty Three

The dreaded day had arrived. Mandy had hardly slept the night before, she had so many mixed emotions. She lay awake thinking about life—past, present, and especially her life in the future. Having baby Macayla brought to her in the morning was a wonderful distraction. She would spend these moments with her instead of focusing on her jumbled thoughts and anxieties.

She dressed baby Macayla in a pink sleeper she had picked up from the store at the Center for Hope. She'd purchased it with her points accumulated from the classes she took there. She loved their selection, and she had found the perfect outfit for Macayla. It was soft pink, and on the left chest was a sweet baby fawn with a bright fuchsia bow between her perked ears. Mandy thought the fawn was fitting for her baby girl's going-home outfit.

It was a fawn Mandy rescued from the hole in her dream. It was Mandy and baby Macayla who had been rescued from the pit of death and despair by Ayala Banks, whose name meant "deer." Had these moments not happened, Mandy would not be at this point in her life. She would not have experienced this new relationship with her Savior, gained the love of her new mother, Mrs. B, or given the gift of life to this little miracle in her arms.

The deer or the symbol of the deer would always hold a special place in Mandy's heart. She believed that the dreams of the doe and the fawn were gifts to her from God. They were His way of guiding her and affirming her in decisions she had made for her and her baby daughter in the last nine months.

And even while under anesthesia during her caesarean section, God guided her in the forest again with His promises. His encouragement and assurance gave her strength to rely on as she woke up to face this day. "Be strong and courageous. Do not be afraid or terrified, for I, the LORD your God, go with you; I will never leave you nor forsake you"—Deuteronomy 31:6 still echoed in her mind. Oh, how she would call on this promise today and the days ahead.

Mandy wrapped Macayla in a matching pink knitted blanket and held her close. She kissed her rosy warm cheeks. She laid her nose against her soft brown curls, closed her eyes, and took in a deep long sniff of her sweetness. "Oh Macayla, I love you so much," she breathed. "I can't wait to see how your life unfolds and the purpose God has for you."

Pulling her closer, she whispered a prayer. "Oh, Father, I pray that Macayla will grow to be a woman of God and bring joy to all she meets. But especially, God, I pray that she will bring joy to You as she lives her life to fulfill the plans You have laid out for her. I know You have big plans for her, God. You've assured me of that over and over. Grow her big and strong and in Your favor, God, and always point her back to You," she prayed over her sweet little daughter as tears fell from her eyes onto Macayla's blanket. Mandy knew she had to pull herself together. She took a tissue from the box on her nightstand with her free hand, dabbed her already swollen eyes, and blew her nose.

She sat on the edge of her hospital bed staring at Macayla, feeling her heartbeat against her own and memorizing her face.

The commotion at the door snapped her out of her trance, and she looked up to see Beth and Mrs. B in the doorway awkwardly pushing a wheelchair.

"Oh, I don't think I need that, I'm perfectly capable of walking," Mandy protested.

"Hospital policy, Missy, not mine," Beth said with a smirk.

Mrs. B rushed over to Mandy's side on the bed. She could see her swollen eyes and wet cheeks. "Are you okay?" she asked as she put her arm around Mandy and her bundle.

"Yes, I'm okay, just full of so many different emotions today. I just want Macayla and me to get on with our future."

Mrs. B ran her hand over Macayla's head and brushed her bent finger down the side of her perfect little face. "I just can't get over how beautiful she is, Mandy!" She squeezed the duo tight to her, and Mandy laid her head on Mrs. B's shoulder. Mrs. B kissed her forehead and whispered, "You've given her life, Mandy. What a blessing she is. What a blessing you are to me, dear daughter!" she added with pride.

Hearing someone call her daughter filled Mandy with a whole new wave of emotion, and she began to sob again, her shoulders shrugging as she sat in Mrs. B's embrace.

Beth was moved to tears as well and bit her bottom lip to try to avoid a full breakdown. "Well, Mandy," she said softly, "we need to get ready to go. They've signed your discharge papers. Do you have your bag packed and ready?"

Rising from her momma bear hug, Mandy said, "Yes, it's over by the closet. I think I have everything." She looked down into sweet baby Macayla's delicate little face again. Mrs. B swept at Mandy's wet face, smoothed her hair, and fussed over her as mothers do.

"Let's do this," she said as she gave Mandy's shoulders one more squeeze.

"I know I don't seem so, but I am ready," Mandy said with renewed strength. "I had another dream. God was clearly showing me the way. He reminded me that He will not leave me, and He will give me courage. And I know He will. I just have to remember that."

She sat down in the wheelchair with baby Macayla in her arms and heaved a sigh. Mrs. B motioned for Beth to come over. "Let's lay our hands on Mandy and baby Macayla and pray over them right now," she suggested as she bent down and opened her arms wide so that she could draw both mother and baby into an embrace. Beth did the same on the other side. The women cried out to God and prayed over mother and child.

Mrs. B led out, "Father God, You have rescued these dear ones. You have given Mandy much courage, wisdom, and strength these last months. You have brought baby Macayla into this world safely and in good health, and we are so thankful for Your provision over them these last days. God, we pray that You will continue to pour out Your blessing on them, that You will carry out the good work that You have called them both to do. Father, give them both what they need right now to face their future with the assurance and comfort that You are with them every step of the way. They can do all things through You, who gives them strength. And God, we pray for extra helpings of strengthening for Mandy now, especially." Her voice began to trail and fill with emotion as Beth started to pray.

"And Father, would You watch over them especially in the days ahead, that their adjustments and transitions in life will go well and that You will keep them both healthy and in Your will. Surround them both with Your people who will love them up and be You in the flesh to them both. Go with us now, Lord, as we leave this place and as Mandy and Macayla move forward. Help Mandy to rest in Your assurance to her. Help her to know, without a shadow of a doubt, that she is giving sweet Macayla the most unselfish act of love she can give. I know that Mandy desires to give Macayla the best she can give, just like You gave us Your best, Your Son, who died on a cross for our sins. God, I pray, that over the days ahead You will give her great peace and comfort and assurance of these things. But most of all, Father, would You please, right now, give us all peace that passes all understanding. Amen." Beth wiped a tear from her eye and hugged Mandy tight.

Mandy was drained; her emotions raw. Even though this was an incredibly emotional time, she had never felt so loved or cared for in her life. She had never felt so sure about anything either.

Mrs. B crammed her soaked tissue into her pocket and wheeled them out. Beth carried Mandy's suitcase and a bag of items the hospital gave her. They rounded the corner and went into a large hospital conference room. As they ventured into the room, Mandy took a deep breath and shot up a silent prayer to God: *Please, Father, help me!* As the wheelchair pushed forward, so did the sudden wave of panic that began to rise in her heart. Remembering the assurance He had given her in the dream, she closed her eyes briefly, took a deep breath and prayed silently, *please rescue Your weak and needy servant, Father!*

She opened her eyes to see Jay and Ruth standing at the back of the room, the couple Mandy had met through a divine appointment God had arranged in the park just a couple of weeks ago. When she accidentally met them that day, she never expected to see them again. She had no idea that they were meeting with Beth the next day to turn in their portfolio to adopt. Even though it was just a chance meeting and she didn't know much about them, Mandy couldn't get them out of her mind after that day. They were kind, fun-loving, and gracious; they were a perfect example of the kind of parents she desired for her daughter. That night she prayed that God would send her a couple like them to adopt her baby.

The next day when Beth mentioned Mandy to the couple, they pulled out the business card that Mandy had left behind the day before and said, "I think we've already met!" When Beth showed up on Mandy's doorstep to deliver a new portfolio for her to consider, she also handed her a gift that the couple wanted to give her. Mandy thought that was odd. *Surely someone hasn't stooped to trying to "buy" my decision with a gift.* She dreaded opening the gift, but when she did, she couldn't believe her eyes. Inside the bag was a pink plastic ball embellished with hearts, just like the one that Jay had accidentally kicked at her in the park, startling her. Attached to the ball was a note: "It appears we might be bumping into you again."

Mandy got weak in the knees. Surely God had provided for her and her baby far better than she could have ever dreamed.

Jay and Ruth were even more incredible when she met with them the next day. They were the couple who made her heart leap with faith. At last, Mandy felt full confidence in her decision to place her baby for adoption. They were perfect in her mind, and she prayed that one day she would know the kind of love and relationship that Jay and Ruth had. They would give her baby a life of love and laughter, and she was happy with them.

And now, at this new meeting with Jay and Ruth, it was apparent to Mandy that they too were filled with an array of emotions. Ruth held her hand to her mouth, and tears streamed from her eyes. Mandy had barely met Ruth, but she felt as if she had known her a lifetime. She was kind, loving, and compassionate; that was what Mandy loved the most about her.

Ruth's tears were a mixture of happy and sad tears, falling together. She felt as sad for Mandy as she felt happy for herself.

Jay was very protective of his sweet wife but protective in the right sense: the way Christ protects his church, with love and gentleness. He stood there with his arm around her thin shoulders, tears streaming down his face, his shoulders shaking with emotion.

They both came running toward Mandy and threw their arms around her, one on each side. Ruth kissed her wet cheek. Her emotions took over, and she was unable to speak. She didn't have to. Mandy understood her language just fine. Jay was no better; he blubbered and clung to Mandy. All five adults in the room were a crying, sobbing mess as baby Macayla slept peacefully in Mandy's arms.

Finally, it was Mandy who lightened the moment. She took a deep breath, sniffed, and cleared her throat. "Jay and Ruth," she said, her voice cracking. The couple pulled themselves away from their embrace and looked Mandy in the eye. "Jay and Ruth," she continued, "I'd like you to meet your daughter! I call her Macayla because it means God's gracious gift." She knew they would understand why this was special to her because she had shared her story with them in detail. "You can name her whatever you want, but to me, she will always be Macayla." She held baby Macayla up to her lips for one last kiss. With every ounce of bravery she could muster, she managed to lay baby Macayla in Ruth's arms.

Time stood still in that moment, and the weight of it would be forever etched in Mandy's memory. It was the most incredibly difficult thing she had ever done, and yet, she was confident she had made the right choice. Never had she loved someone this much. It was a fierce love that gave Mandy the courage to dig down deep into her selfish heart and give baby Macayla the most unselfish act of love she could provide.

Ruth looked down into Macayla's face, and now her tears began to intermingle with Mandy's on the baby's pink blanket. Jay was at her side, his cheeks wet. He pulled his hanky from his pocket and ran it over his face. He peered down at the bundle in his wife's arms. "She's the most beautiful baby I've ever seen, Mandy!" he exclaimed with a big dimply smile.

Ruth managed to speak through her crying, "Oh, Mandy, she's beautiful. I love her name. I love the meaning of it and its importance to you. Macayla it shall be. Macayla Rose after my grandmother Rose!" Ruth said proudly. "Mandy, we will love her like crazy. We promise to give her the best life we can. Lots of people will love her. There's a whole bunch of people waiting to meet her and love up on her!"

"Is Loopity Loo Lucy one of them?" Mandy interrupted the emotional moment with a chuckle.

Ruth gave Mandy a big grin. "Oh Yes, Lucy is so excited to have a girl cousin to play with!"

Ruth was able to keep her composure long enough to tell Mandy what was on her heart: "Thank you, Mandy, for giving her the gift of life. And thank you for giving us the gift of her."

The enormity of the sacrifice made on her behalf came crashing down on Ruth, and there was no controlling the emotion that welled up inside of her now. As grateful as she was to call this sweet child her daughter, she recognized how incredibly hard it must be for Mandy to say goodbye to her. At this moment, joy and sorrow walked hand in hand, and Ruth shared in Mandy's grief. She was humbled and filled with love for this woman who had entrusted her with a mother's most valuable treasure.

Jay wept uncontrollably, and all he could do was put his hand on Mandy's shoulder.

Mandy reached up and touched Jay's hand. He didn't have to say anything. She understood gratitude. Over the last several months she had experienced it in more ways than she could count. She understood his love for this child. She couldn't have done what she was doing if she didn't love Macayla so much. She knew that this choice for Macayla was the best choice. She knew she could not give her much of a life, nor was she ready to. Mandy had a lot of maturing and growing to do herself. She had just begun the healing process of a very broken life, and her future was still uncertain. She knew that Macayla needed and deserved much more. She needed stability, and Ruth and Jay were the perfect couple to provide that. More than anything in the world, Ruth and Jay desired to parent a child, and she knew that Macayla would be parented well, with godly guidance. Ruth and Jay needed Macayla as much as she needed them.

Mandy was moved by how they adored Macayla already. She admired how they loved each other, how much they loved Jesus— and how much they loved her.

Eventually, the stream of tears slowed down, and Beth was able to talk to them all about keeping Mandy updated on Macayla's progress throughout the years. Ruth and Jay asked if they could all pray together. Mandy stood up from her wheelchair, and they all stood arm in arm to pray.

Both Ruth and Jay hugged Mandy and, this time, Mandy gave Macayla one final kiss. The warmth of her cheek would forever be on her lips. She said her goodbyes, and they left. And with them went Mandy's heart.

CHAPTER
Thirty Four

Mandy threw an extra sweater in her suitcase. Rae had warned her of the chilly Minnesota evenings this time of year. An extra pair of jeans would probably be a good idea too, Mandy told herself as she pulled a pair from her drawer. It felt good to be able to zip up her old jeans again. The last traces of her pregnancy were finally firming up, and her body was slowly healing and getting back into shape.

Although she was glad to have her old body back, she found she had become oddly comforted by the little bulge left behind the last several weeks. It served as the only physical reminder of sweet baby Macayla, who had not only grown underneath her heart for nine months but in her heart as well.

The last eleven months of her life had been difficult, but this two-month period after Macayla's birth was by far the hardest thing she had ever experienced. She found herself crying at the oddest times and for the strangest reasons. She missed feeling Macayla move inside her and having a connection with her. The wonderful feeling of life growing within her had been replaced with the dull ache of a broken heart.

Even though Macayla was alive and well, in the last eight weeks Mandy had been going through a real grieving process. When she'd made the final decision to place her for adoption, she knew it would be tough, and some days, admittedly, were worse than others. She had been meeting with Beth and her pastor each week, getting counsel from them both in how to deal with her grief.

Mandy had already received several updates on Macayla's progress from Jay and Ruth. She was sure that if Jay could pull the moon out of the sky, he would lasso it and give it to his sweet baby girl. They adored Macayla. And even though the pictures of them together brought tears to her eyes, she would never have done things differently. She loved them all too much for that. Macayla was being nurtured, cared for, and loved in ways that she couldn't even imagine. They were giving Macayla the life she had always dreamed of for herself; the same life she had hoped and prayed for Macayla. She especially loved the pictures of Jay and Macayla together, as Mandy had never known what it was to have a dad. She was grateful to God for providing both a loving mother and father for her daughter. Of course, Cousin Lucy made her way into the photos also, and Mandy always smiled when she saw the joy on Lucy's face as she held the pink bundle.

She was grieving, yes, but her thankfulness for God's provision over Macayla and her peace with her adoption plan far outweighed her grief. Repeatedly, Jay and Ruth thanked her for giving them this gift in the letters they sent. But Mandy felt Jay and Ruth had given her an incredible gift—that of offering her baby girl a most amazing life, which Mandy was not able to offer currently in her journey.

Even though some days in her healing process were harder than others, Mandy was moving forward. She had been through many disappointments and heartaches in her lifetime, but this time it was different. This time she didn't go it alone. She had a host of support around her to help her through. Mandy wasn't just healing from her grief but recovering from a lifetime of wounds. Many of those wounds were still fresh for her, but slowly, thanks to so many who were loving her up with Jesus's love, the scabs were falling off, and new growth was forming.

Having Macayla was the best thing to happen to her. It was because of Macayla that she had found Jesus, Mrs. B, and hope! Pretty soon she would also have a new last name as she became Mandy Banks, officially Ayala Banks's daughter. At last she had a real family. Both Mandy and Macayla had been gifted by God with wonderful, godly mothers. She looked at this name change as a clean slate, a new beginning. The last several months had proven to be a real metamorphosis for her, and she was ready to spread her wings and fly into new experiences without the shame and disappointments of her past keeping her coiled up in a cocoon of bitterness.

In a couple of weeks, she would begin a new job as a receptionist at the Center for Hope. She remembered what Beth had told her once about not wasting her suffering. That had left a lasting impression on her. She hoped God would be able to use this pain in her life to help girls at the pregnancy resource center to have hope and choose life for their babies. She would have not only a job but also an outlet for ministry. Being with the godly women who worked there would also help Mandy as she continued to heal, grow, and mature in her spiritual journey as well. She prayed that God would use her story someday to rescue a life, just as He had used Mrs. B's story to rescue her and Macayla.

Mrs. B's ministry was already going strong, and they had another girl living with them. She attended the university, and her parents had cut her off because of her pregnancy. Mrs. B ministered to her as she had so graciously done for Mandy and Rae. Mrs. B was keeping a room open for Mandy until she was ready to venture out on her own and regain her independence. There was no hurry though, as they were enjoying their time as mother and daughter.

Mandy looked forward to Wednesday evening Bible study alongside her new mom. She wanted to just sit at Ayala Banks's feet and glean wisdom from her 24-7. Mrs. B had taught Mandy much about being a woman after God's own heart. She loved the church she was attending with Mrs. B, and plans were under way for her baptism in a few weeks.

She was discovering how good her God really was, and at times, she was overwhelmed thinking about all the amazing ways He had worked in her life these last months. He was a God who revealed Himself to her in dreams and helped her have peace in troubled times. He was a God who used nighttime adventures to convince her that He was worthy of her trust. He had guided her, comforted her, and strengthened her through these dreams. She was learning to lean on Him. Just as she had leaned on Him in her forest dream quest to find a home for the lost fawn, He had shown her He could be trusted to find baby Macayla's home as well.

She no longer had her recurring dream. The dream had ended with four does coming to her and the fawn's rescue. It ended the way Mandy's new life had begun over this last year. She also was given the gift of four nurturing women to help her find her way when she was lost. Mrs. B, Rae, Beth, and Ruth had all taught her about unselfish love and where that love comes from. God had proven to her time and again that His ways were perfect, and His plans were sure. Her trust in Him continued to be a work in progress.

She tried to remember this when her old way of thinking reared its ugly head. Sometimes in the stillness and darkness of night, the bitterness of her past, the fear of the future, and the disappointment of her old life would haunt her. In her healing process, she was learning how to cope with all the feelings that came from darkness. She was learning to take baby steps into the light. Each day was a day of hope and healing for Mandy as she chose to move forward and walk in the light of Christ's love.

She closed her suitcase and zipped it shut. She noticed a card in a bright blue envelope that lay next to her suitcase on the bed. She smiled when she saw it. It was the birth announcement she had received a couple of weeks ago and the reason she was packing her suitcase. She and Mrs. B had snickered when Mandy pulled the card from the mailbox and saw "Your little Rae of Sunshine" was handwritten in the return address spot. They knew it was from Rae, and they couldn't wait to rip it open. Mandy opened it again and held the photo card in her hand. There was her beautiful friend, Rae, looking more radiant than ever with her red curls cascading across her shoulders. Skylar sat snuggled up beside her with a proud grin on his face. In her arms, she cradled the cutest baby with a tuft of red hair atop his round head.

The rest of the card announced the birth of Skylar Ross Weaver Jr. and all his important stats. Alongside the announcement was a personal note to her and Ayala, inviting them to a baby shower and celebration of life for little Ross.

Mandy pulled the brightly colored gift she had wrapped for baby Ross and set it neatly on top of her suitcase. As soon as Mrs. B returned from a meeting, they would head out to Minnesota. They were going to take their time and make a vacation out of it, their first mother-daughter adventure of many to come. In fact it was Mandy's first vacation ever, her first time out of the state. Mall of America, of course, was on their agenda, but what they really looked forward to was snuggling with baby Ross and hugging Rae's neck.

Mandy had great things to look forward to in life. Hope was on the horizon. "One day at a time," Mrs. B reminded Mandy whenever she was feeling apprehensive or overwhelmed. It was a principle Mandy had once adopted out of necessity in her life, but now she was really applying it. One day at a time used to mean surviving the moment. But now it meant truly living in the moment. The old Mandy seldom had anything to look forward to; the new Mandy found herself waiting in expectation of the next great thing. For the first time in her life, she wasn't just wandering through life; she was finding purpose.

She was slowly adjusting to the foreign idea of belonging. Being part of a greater plan was daunting yet exciting. Naturally, withdrawing and allowing life to just happen around her was most comfortable. She understood now how much she had missed by shutting others out of her life. She was boldly taking steps out of her comfort zone and into the arms of God's people.

Placing the baby fawn with the welcoming does in the meadow, she had experienced great peace knowing God had guided her to the place where he belonged. Like the baby fawn, Mandy had assurance that baby Macayla was also where she belonged, loved by her doting parents. And here, in this place, filled with His spirit, welcomed by His people, at long last, Mandy belonged.

Mrs. B had bought Mandy the *Message* version of the Bible to help her understand some passages better. She loved reading from it; it was like reading poetry. She hungered for more and more of God's word. His words were a balm to her soul and a light to her path, these last few months especially. Every time she read or discussed the scriptures with others, she fell more in love with her Savior.

She headed toward the living room to grab her copy of *The Message* to take on the trip. She found it there next to Mrs. B's morning devotion book. It was open to Ephesians 2 with verses 19–22 highlighted:

> That's plain enough, isn't it? You're no longer wandering exiles. This kingdom of faith is now your home country. You're no longer strangers or outsiders. You belong here, with as much right to the name Christian as anyone. God is building a home. He's using us all—irrespective of how we got here—in what he is building. He used the apostles and prophets for the foundation. Now he's using you, fitting you in brick by brick, stone by stone, with Christ Jesus as the cornerstone that holds all the parts together. We see it taking shape day after day—a holy temple built by God, all of us built into it, a temple in which God is quite at home.

In the margin, written big and bold in Mrs. B's loopy cursive, was Mandy's name. Below it was a special message meant for her eyes to see: "Welcome home, my dear daughter, welcome home!"

Printed and bound by PG in the USA

USA2016PG1L